Also by Kathryn Gualtieri

Murder in the Pines
(A Nora Finnegan Mystery)

Half Moon Bay: Birth of a Coastside Town

MURDER TAKES THE STAGE

Kathryn Gualtieri

Murder Takes the Stage is a work of fiction, whose story-line and characters are the products of the author's imagination, but woven around incidents that occurred in early Carmel history. See Author's Note at the end of the novel.

Modified cover photograph and other photographs are credited to the Henry Meade Williams Local History Department, Harrison Memorial Library, Carmel, California. Cover silhouette by Kay Holz.

A Tin Lantern Publication
Post Office Box 1483
Capitola, California 95010

Book design by Dorothy Foglia,
Aptos, California

Printed in the United States of America.

ISBN 978-0-615-70552-1

This novel is dedicated to Herbert Heron. (photo above)
His vision inspired the creation of the outdoor Forest Theater
in 1910 as a community tradition that, more than any
other project, continues to evoke the essence and beauty
of Carmel-By-The-Sea.

CHAPTER ONE

Carmel-By-The-Sea, California

Friday, July 21, 1922

Grim-faced and angry, *Carmel Pine Cone* reporter Nora Finnegan pounded the keys of her Underwood. Why had her boss insisted that she stay past quitting time, when he knew she would be late for play rehearsal? How cruel and inconsiderate of him! She bemoaned the fact there were still occasions like this one when she must accept that her job had no schedule. Even so, it did have its limits.

Just then, the door to the newspaper publisher's office banged open and William Owens stepped out. Looking around the empty reception area, he said, "I'm struck by all this clutter, Honora." Having known her since her birth twenty-two years ago, Owens persisted in calling Nora by her given name.

She stopped typing and glanced up. Her blue eyes glared at him.

Hovering near her desk, he said, "What are those stacks of newspapers doing on the floor and unfilled customers' orders piled up on the front counter?"

When she didn't answer, he continued, "Mrs. Owens always

takes care of things immediately. While she's out of town, you're supposed to cover her office duties. The least you can do is to stay on top of it."

For a brief moment, Nora almost felt sorry for the man. His shoulders sagged, as if carrying a heavy burden. Stubble on his normally clean-shaven face had aged him beyond his forty years. A green eyeshade, smudged with recent fingerprints, sat askew at the back of his head.

Before she could say anything, he continued his diatribe. "Have you finished your story on the new post office dedication? I plan to typeset it before leaving tonight."

"I'm working on it."

"Make sure you add the titles of all the politicians and local dignitaries who were at the ceremony this afternoon."

Nora was irked. "I've always done that since I started working here a year ago. I know the importance of getting people's names into every article I write." Checking the wall clock, she added, "I'm nearly done, Mr. Owens, and I'm due at the theater in fifteen minutes. Our director doesn't tolerate tardiness."

"I'm the one who's paying your salary, not James Carpenter."

"Why are you so grouchy?" she countered. "If I'm late, I'll have to change out of my business suit and into my costume somewhere else besides the Forest Theater's dressing room. Mr. Carpenter doesn't allow anyone downstairs once rehearsal starts."

"There's always the bathroom down the hall."

Nora grimaced. She didn't much care for the idea of using a semi-public facility that the *Pine Cone* staff shared with customers of the art gallery next door. Besides, she would have to wear her maid's uniform all the way to the theater, and be forced to tolerate the furtive glances and head shakings from her fellow Carmelites as she traipsed through the village.

Shrugging his shoulders, as if to say, 'That's just the way it is,' Owens busied himself rustling some papers at the reception desk and then walked back to his office.

Nora finished typing her article. Already late, she got up and went to change in the dreaded bathroom. Returning to her desk, she put together the pages of her story and headed for the publisher's office. Knocking, but not opening Owens' closed door, she shouted, "I'll leave my article on the front counter. Good night."

As she walked back to her desk, the telephone rang. Picking it up, she said, "*Carmel Pine Cone*. Miss Finnegan speaking."

"It's Claudia Jacklin, Nora. I'm glad I caught you. I won't be walking with you to rehearsal tonight. Freddie came down with a fever and an upset stomach."

"That's too bad. Let's hope he's feeling better by tomorrow. I know how much that boy looks forward to playing softball on the weekends. Shall I tell our director that you aren't coming?"

"No, you won't have to. I telephoned Vera and she's delighted to inform James that I won't be there. After cozying up to him and landing the understudy part, the little vamp can move on and bat her artificial eyelashes at our handsome leading man."

Nora laughed. "You've been seeing too many Theda Bara movies."

"You know me too well. Listen, I've got to go. Freddie's calling. I'll see you tomorrow at the softball field and you can tell me how rehearsal went without me."

As Nora bent down to retrieve her purse from her desk's bottom drawer, William Owens opened his office door. She could hear him muttering to himself. Hands in his pockets, shirt sleeves rolled up to his elbows, he headed over to her desk.

"I owe you an apology, Honora," he said. "I'm sure you've noticed that I haven't been myself since taking Mary Lee and Sally to the train station last Saturday. I've had to work extra hours since they left, and still I can't keep up. The truth is, I'm miserable without my wife and daughter, to the point where I hate going home to an empty house tonight."

Nora's anger cooled. "I know what you mean. I miss them too." More so now than ever, she thought. Not only was she filling in as the *Pine Cone*'s receptionist, but the publisher's wife usually took her side in disagreements. "I'm really late, Mr. Owens," she said. "I'm leaving now, but I'll be in at noon tomorrow."

Grinning at her as she reached for the door handle, he teased, "Don't wear that maid's outfit when we make the rounds of the merchants. I guarantee they won't be able to concentrate on their weekly advertising copy."

Nora felt certain that Mrs. Owens would have poked her husband in the ribs for his comment. She waved without looking back at him.

As she hurried along Ocean Avenue, Carmel's business district, Nora sensed that passersby were staring at her. Were they reacting to her silly costume, or was it because her long legs were uncovered just above her knees? Reaching the base of the hill that led to the coastal road, she turned right and headed up Mountain View Avenue. Making her way through the pine trees at the perimeter of the theater, the starched cap perched on her curly black hair snagged on a low-hanging branch. Even nature was conspiring to delay her. Coming up behind the stage, she took the wooden steps two at a time. She heard loud voices on the other side of the backdrop. From the conversations, she realized that rehearsal hadn't begun. She was on time.

Tiptoeing to the other side of the stage, she came up to her serving cart and noticed there was something odd about it. The Chintzware teapot, sugar bowl, cups and saucers were all together on the silver tray, but the matching cream pitcher was sitting off to the side. Burt Erickson was getting more and more forgetful, she thought. She rearranged the tea service as the prop man should have done, and was relieved that none of the milk that Burt had poured into the pitcher had spilled.

Positioning herself and the cart at stage left, she called out to James Carpenter, to let him know that she was there. Middle-aged, and wearing a broad-brimmed Panama hat, the play's author and director was seated by himself in the center section of the front row. Intent on stroking his trimmed beard with one hand while turning pages of the script with the other, he looked up, nodded, and waved at her. Then he motioned to the young stagehand standing nearby to ignite the piles of freshly cut logs in the fire pits on either side of the outdoor stage.

Nora was grateful for some heat. Her skimpy outfit was ill-suited to the quickly dropping temperature. It was twilight, and even with the fire pits blazing below, summer nights were always cool. While she waited, she stared out at the empty, open-air amphitheater, built a dozen years ago by a group of local playwrights and poets. She felt at home in the intimate forest setting and relished living in a place where theater was a treasured community event. Tonight she joined other residents with regular daytime jobs who, like herself, looked forward to acting in the evenings.

In a week's time, excited families, their picnic baskets and blankets in tow, would file in and fill the rows of wooden benches creeping step-wise up the natural sloping embankment surrounded by tall pines. Nora could imagine the opening night of "A Shadow Falls on Justice," when an appreciative crowd would acknowledge her and her fellow cast members with a bevy of curtain calls.

Her eyes scanned the stage and its parlor scene painted on makeshift walls. The lead actor, Guy Porter, dressed in a double-breasted suit, and playing the role of a criminal defense attorney, was sitting on a sofa facing the audience. A tall, dark-haired, square-jawed man in his late twenties, he had been brought in by the director for the part. At auditions two months ago, Nora learned that James Carpenter had recruited Guy from a professional theater company in San Francisco, after meeting him at the Bohemian Club. Already, there were murmurs among Carmelites who were critical of the outsider. All the other actors the director had chosen were local residents.

In a nearby armchair, playing the role of a retired army colonel accused of murder, sat Randall King. A seasoned local actor, Nora knew he worked part-time as a waiter at the Pine Inn. Since her teenage years, she had idolized him. Now in his forties, she thought his graying hair and trimmed mustache made him look distinguished. Pulling a pipe from a pocket of his tweed jacket, Randall lit it and took several long puffs. If only he were a few years younger, she fantasized.

Seated in a matching armchair across from Randall was Vera Winfield, Claudia Jacklin's understudy. Tonight she would be playing the role of the colonel's wife. A slender, yet curvaceous redhead, her bobbed hair, arched brows, and copious eye makeup accented her hazel eyes. Luckily, Vera fitted easily into Claudia's costume: a gray velveteen suit embroidered with two rows of jet black beads down the jacket's front.

Nora watched in amazement as the young actress glanced over at Guy and winked at him, then rolled her tongue over her lips. Claudia had been right in calling her a "little vamp," she thought. Vera Winfield was making a play for the leading man's attention.

Clapping his hands, the director shouted, "Places, everyone. Begin Act One."

Waiting for her cue, Nora listened to Guy's commanding, baritone voice.

DEFENSE ATTORNEY: *(Speaking forcefully)* I tell you, Colonel, the argument you want me to present in court isn't going to convince anyone of your innocence. You're a war hero. I urge you to testify on your own behalf. I am absolutely certain that you will impress the jury.

COLONEL: *(Shaking his head)* I don't want to be cross-examined by the prosecutor. I told you that, when you agreed to defend me. It's too risky. *(Takes a puff from his pipe)* He will twist my words and contradict what I say. I'll be convicted of a crime I didn't commit.

DEFENSE ATTORNEY: *(Leaning forward with somber emphasis)* I insist you change your mind, Colonel. Perhaps a discussion of the alternatives is in order. Let's have a little tea before we proceed. *(He turns and waves at the maid standing to his left at the rear of the room.)* You may serve us now, Dottie.

MAID: *(Pushes her serving cart to mid stage and positions it next to the sofa where the attorney is seated)* Everything's ready, sir.

DEFENSE ATTORNEY: *(Looks at the colonel)* I take mine with cream.

COLONEL: *(Straightens up and puts his pipe in an ashtray on a side table)* Two lumps of sugar in mine. *(Looks at wife)* And what would you like in yours, dear?

COLONEL'S WIFE: *(Smiles at the maid)* Give me one lump only, please.

Suddenly, Randall sprang out of his chair and yelled, "Look out!"

Nora jumped instinctively, as Guy rolled over and dropped to the floor, just as a section of newly-painted wall behind them toppled and landed on top of the sofa.

Stepping forward, Randall lifted the heavy piece of wallboard off the sofa, with the help of the stagehand.

In the confusion, Vera got up and went to kneel beside the

fallen actor. "Are you all right, Guy?" she asked. Putting out her hand, she tentatively touched his shoulder. "Is anything broken?"

"Yes, something's broken, Vera," he said in a stern voice. "What's broken is my faith in this amateur theater company." Getting to his feet, he brushed off his clothing and ran a hand through his tousled hair. He turned to the director, who had climbed up on stage. "I've never worked under such primitive conditions, James. I'm ready to quit your play and return to San Francisco."

"Calm down," the director replied. "This is the first time Burt didn't secure a piece of scenery. He probably forgot to fix it to the floor after repainting it last night. I'll talk to him and make sure it doesn't happen again. Now let's resume rehearsal."

"I don't feel like it," Guy said. "I'm having a cigarette instead." Pushing past Randall and Vera, he stormed off the stage.

To Nora's relief, she was unhurt and her tea service was intact. However, she was surprised by Guy's threat. Yes, he had been frightened, but why had he needed to demean Carmel's theater program?

Standing next to her, Vera whispered, "Guy might have been badly hurt and of course, you too, Nora. I think Burt should be fired. He could be drinking again."

Nora shook her head. "I don't think so. James warned him about that last week. Burt will get a talking-to, but I doubt he'll be dismissed so close to opening night."

As the words rolled off her tongue, Nora realized that she hadn't told the director about the prop man's failure to prepare her tea tray correctly.

But it was too late. James had disappeared back stage, on his way to admonish the negligent Burt.

CHAPTER TWO

"Erickson!" James Carpenter shouted. Not waiting for a reply, the director approached the low outbuilding at the rear of the theater where the play's sets were stored. Stepping into semi-darkness, he edged forward among the scenery, costume racks, and stacks of paint cans. When he reached the workbench, he stared down at Burt Erickson. His hair matted with blood, the prop man was lying on his side on the dirt floor. Crouching next to him, James nudged his shoulder and turned him over.

Raising his hand to his scalp, Burt moaned, "My head is splitting."

"What happened? Have you been drinking? Remember, I warned you about that."

"No, sir. I was standing right here, James. I've been working on that justice scale you wanted polished. I got whacked from behind."

"Did you see who it was?"

Closing his eyes, Burt turned away and responded with a shrug.

"I'll get you some help," the director said.

Observing the play's interrupted rehearsal from the Forest Theater's eighth row, Victor Wolfe, Guy Porter's understudy, waited until he saw the director reappear. When James reached the front of the stage, Victor left his seat and sauntered down the aisle.

Lanky, with deep-set eyes and a full head of straight black hair parted on one side, Victor had enjoyed witnessing the scenery collapse on his rival. Since the auditions, he had chafed over the director's decision to select an outsider for the play's leading part. Victor hoped Guy would now refuse to go on, and he would be tapped to replace him. "Can I help you, James?" he called out, as he stepped off the bottom stair.

"That's very thoughtful of you, Victor. Would you head over to that cottage across the street and ask to use the telephone? I want you to call the doctor and tell him we have an emergency. Burt's had an accident."

Victor hated being anyone's lackey, but he knew better than to refuse the request. Nodding, he said, "Doc Barnes works most nights, seeing patients. I'll try him at home first. If he's making house calls, I'll track him down."

Patting Victor's shoulder as the young man went past him, James turned and rejoined the rest of the cast on stage.

Listening to their conversation, Vera Winfield said, "How badly hurt is he, James?"

"He sustained a nasty blow to his head, but he'll be O.K."

Looking concerned, Vera continued, "I hope what's happened won't discourage Guy from staying on and working with us."

Just then, Randall King came up to join them. "In my humble opinion, Victor can fill the bill. Yes, he lacks Guy's training and experience, but he has some talent, James. Giving him the leading man's part will have the added benefit of placating the Forest Theater Society's members. I'm sure you've heard that they're all pretty miffed about your bringing in a professional actor."

"You seem to forget that this is my original play, Randall,

and it won this year's competition," James shot back. "I have the right to select my own actors."

Standing near the others, Nora remembered something that supported Randall's contention. Perry Newberry, an active member of the Society, and a longtime resident, had castigated James Carpenter in a scathing letter to the *Carmel Pine Cone*. Perry had publicly called the director's action "shocking and unforgiveable." Rumor had it that he was encouraging his fellow Carmelites to boycott James' play on opening night.

A noise caused Nora to turn her head. Guy reappeared on stage. He sauntered over to her serving cart and poured himself some milk from the pitcher on the tray. Lifting the teacup to his mouth, he took several long swallows.

Nora's eyes widened on seeing what happened next.

Guy's face became frozen. His jaws clenched, and suddenly, a projectile of milk exploded from his open mouth. Grabbing at his throat with both hands, he began coughing. The teacup dropped to the floor and shattered. Guy fell to his knees and continued coughing and choking.

Not quite knowing what to do, Nora didn't move until Randall pushed past her and began hitting his fellow actor on the back.

Waving his hand to ward off the blows, Guy gasped, "Water!"

Randall scrambled off the stage to a nearby water spigot with an attached hose. Turning it on, he pitched the hose nozzle onto the stage, so that Guy could reach it. The actor jammed it in his mouth and drank.

Nora knelt down next to Guy and brushed away some of the larger pieces of broken china. Suddenly, she exclaimed, "Something has eaten a hole in the carpet."

Rushing over to inspect the damage, Vera looked down. Her face paled. "Nora, whatever did you add to that milk?"

Nora's face reddened as the director joined them. "I had nothing to do with this, James," she said. "As you know, Burt always prepares the tea set for me."

Breathing heavily and dripping water from his head and face, Guy struggled to his feet. "Fire him, James. Whether you do or not, I'm still holding you culpable for the damage this does to my acting career."

"Be rational, man. I'll get to the bottom of this, and you're going to be just fine."

Nora interrupted, "I don't think this was an accident, James. You need to call in Marshal Englund."

"A marshal?" Guy's voice rasped. "No small town constable will be able to figure this out. Call the Pinkerton Detective Agency in San Francisco."

James shook his head. "There's no need for that. Nora's right. Our local lawman has the authority to investigate the assault on Burt and also figure out how a foreign substance got into the cream pitcher."

"I agree," Randall said. "We don't want any negative publicity whatsoever. It could reflect badly on us and our play. And it would only fuel more criticism from Perry Newberry and the rest of the members of the Forest Theater Society."

"You needn't be concerned about the marshal's investigative abilities, Guy," Nora interjected. "Before coming to work in Carmel, Gus Englund was Monterey's police chief and before that, he was a Pinkerton agent himself. He's very competent." She didn't add that the marshal had rescued her from near death last November, as she lay exhausted and helpless on Carmel Beach.

Motioning to Randall, James said, "Go telephone the marshal and explain what's happened. When the doctor gets here, I'll make sure he takes a good look at your throat, Guy — as soon as he's finished treating Burt's head wound."

Guy's voice sounded ragged. "He won't have the medical expertise to evaluate my injuries. I need a specialist, and until I get one, I'm not working here again."

"You should rest until Doc Barnes can see you, Guy," Vera put in. "I'll take you back to the dressing room so you can lie down for a while."

Offering no resistance, the actor said, "Would you help me downstairs, Vera?"

As she watched the couple link arms and slowly walk off stage, Nora wondered if someone connected to the Forest Theater Society was trying to put an end to their play. If so, all of Carmel's residents would be caught up in this controversy.

CHAPTER THREE

Never having stepped onto the Forest Theater's outdoor stage before, Marshal Gus Englund felt out of place. He had faced many crime scenes in his time, but never one in such a serene forest setting. The calcium floodlights that had once illuminated the earliest plays here had now been replaced by a string of electric lights overhead. He gazed down at the assembled group seated in the front row — all familiar faces, innocent, but expectant. Like birds perched on a wire, he mused.

Sitting with her fellow cast members, Nora wondered if the marshal had ever performed in any play. He was a handsome man in a rugged sort of way. She guessed him to be somewhere in his mid-fifties. Tall and fair-haired with a medium build, his broad shoulders and ramrod posture called to mind his past military training. But as intimidating as his physical presence was, she had to smile at his obvious bow-legged stance. She figured that it stemmed from his cavalry stint in the U. S. Army.

The marshal turned and reached for one of the chairs in the parlor scene. Picking it up with one hand, he carried it to the edge of the stage, sat down, and crossed his arms over his chest.

He was about to speak when Randall, seated on one side of Nora, stood up and removed his tweed jacket. Holding it out to her, he said, "We can't have you freezing to death in that skimpy maid's costume. This should keep you warm while we're being interviewed."

Nodding her thanks, Nora took the jacket and draped it over her shoulders. As she settled back on the wood bench, she felt an elbow nudging her.

Vera, who was sitting on her other side, leaned closer and whispered, "He's such a considerate man. If only Guy were that attentive to me."

Marshal Englund's voice boomed out, "Here's what we know. Someone has assaulted Burt Erickson. And somebody's put a dangerous substance into a cream pitcher. Maybe the incidents are connected. Maybe not. Now I'm going to need your help. I'll be questioning you as a group first, but I'll follow up individually with some of you tomorrow. For that reason, nobody is to leave Carmel until I say so. Is that clear?"

Nora looked down the bench and noticed that everyone was nodding, even Victor, who had just come from back stage and seated himself next to Vera.

"Can you start with me, sir? My ma worries when I get home late," Tommy Anderson called out. The stagehand was standing at the end of the aisle nearest the exit.

Blonde-haired, of average height, and with a stocky frame, Nora knew him from his work around the newspaper office. Mr. Owens had felt sorry for Tommy and paid him to deliver the weekly papers throughout the village.

"All right, young man," the marshal said. "I remember you. We've met up with each other quite a few times in the past when you were out of line."

Tommy's face broke into a lopsided grin. "Yes, we sure have, Marshal. You got me out of several scrapes in high school and I'm thankful for that."

"I guess I did, son. So why don't you start by telling me

what time you got here today and what are your duties?"

"I came at four o'clock, sir. That's when my shift starts on the days when there's a play rehearsal. I take down the scenery the other crew from the Forest Theater Society uses and sweep the stage floor clean." Pointing to the cast members, he added, "I put up the new scenery before these people show up at five o'clock."

Nora could see that the marshal was somewhat perplexed by Tommy's answer.

"You mean to tell me that two different theater groups use this same stage on the same night?" Englund asked. "Sounds like I might have to interrogate more people."

At the far end of the row, James, the play's director, piped up. "You have to know that Carmel has very limited space when it comes to live theater venues, Marshal."

"Sounds like maybe you need another place to perform."

James nodded. "I couldn't agree with you more. In a real pinch, we can use the Carmel Club of Arts and Crafts, but it's usually booked up with other events besides plays. It's always a challenge, since we in the Western Drama Society have to share this outdoor stage with Herbert Heron and his Forest Theater company. We've been lucky to work out an arrangement that satisfies both of us."

The marshal nodded and then looked at the stagehand, to pick up where he had left off. "O.K., Tommy, while you were doing your chores this afternoon, did you by any chance see anybody you didn't know wandering around the theater?"

Tommy stared at the smoldering fire pit in front of him, as if he might find an answer in the crackling embers. Finally he looked up and said, "No, sir, there was nobody that didn't belong here."

As if he were expecting that response, the marshal went on, "Did your duties take you into the building where Burt works?"

Nora saw Tommy staring down at the ground, shifting his weight from one foot to the other. She wondered if he might be trying to conceal something.

After a deep sigh, he looked up at the marshal. "When I first got here, I went out back to return some scenery from the other play and I picked up the kindling for the fire pits. The shed door was wide open and I could see Burt at his bench. He was polishing up those brass scales for Mr. Carpenter. I went inside and we talked for a while."

"How long were you in the prop room?" Englund probed.

"Can't say for sure — maybe five minutes? I don't have a watch. Look, I didn't hurt him, Marshal, if that's what you're getting at. I swear, he was just fine when I left."

"No one's accusing you of assaulting Burt. Doctor Barnes has examined him. He's keeping an eye on him and he thinks he'll be all right. You've just helped me figure out that he was attacked after you two talked, and before this group's rehearsal started sometime before five o'clock."

Randall jumped to his feet. "When are you going to get to the real problem, sir? It's pretty clear that somebody has tried to poison us."

Englund held up his hand. "I was just getting to that."

Fidgeting in her seat, Nora was eager to tell the marshal about Burt's misplacing the cream pitcher, when the marshal pointed his finger at Randall.

"Since you interrupted me, Mr. King, let me ask you something. I know you've performed in lots of plays put on by the Forest Theater Society over the last dozen years or so. I've attended most of them and I've always admired your talent. What puzzles me is why you've suddenly switched your allegiance from Mr. Heron's group to Mr. Carpenter's Western Drama Society?"

"That's a personal matter that I don't care to discuss."

"Not so. This is a police matter. I'm looking for a motive. I want an answer."

Sinking down on the bench, Randall lowered his voice and continued talking. "For the past year, I've been increasing my savings by taking on more work. I want to move to a place like Hollywood, where actors are paid a decent wage. On the nights when I don't perform, I wait tables at the Pine Inn. I also chauffeur people who hire me through Pete Quinlan's garage. I take any kind of job that's offered to me."

"All that sounds admirable, but there's still the question of your misplaced loyalty to the Forest Theater Society," the marshal said. "When I arrived here tonight, I was told by Mr. Carpenter that a heavy piece of scenery had collapsed onstage. I know you actors are competitive and jealous of one another. Do you think someone is sending the Western Drama Society a warning, Mr. King?"

The actor shrugged his shoulders. "How should I know? The fallen backdrop was an accident, pure and simple. Burt or Tommy should have noticed it and taken care of it."

All eyes, including Nora's, looked at Tommy, who, by now, was squirming in his seat.

"But the tainted milk was no accident," Randall persisted. "Burt was in charge of that too. Why don't you question him?"

"I'll be talking to Burt when he's well enough," the marshal said.

Vera waved her arm and stood up. "Excuse me, Marshal, but I might be the target, just as much as Guy. We're both from San Francisco and we came here at the invitation of James Carpenter. My loyalty could be questioned too."

"You might be right," Englund said, "but don't worry, young lady. I'll sort things out, with a little time. Please take your seat. I'd like to get on with this."

Nora was about to raise her hand and say her piece, when a

husky male voice interrupted her.

"I'd like to add something to this discussion."

All eyes turned to watch Guy Porter make his way down the aisle between the stage and the front row bench. Pausing in front of the marshal, he looked up at the lawman. "I've just been examined by Doctor Barnes in the dressing room. He says that I have a bad burn in my throat."

As she listened to the sound of Guy's voice, Nora wondered if the actor would be fit to continue in the play's leading role. His clear baritone timber had disappeared.

Guy grabbed hold of the edge of the stage for support. "Marshal, you need to contact a Pinkerton detective. Get him to come down here from San Francisco."

James Carpenter interjected, "Please, Guy. Let him do his job."

Englund squared his shoulders. "You don't know how things work around here, Mr. Porter. I'll decide if I need help. Since I'm the one asking the questions, here's one for you. As a newcomer to this community, has anyone attempted to threaten you?"

Guy slowly moved over to the bench and sat down between Randall and the director before answering. "Why don't you ask him?" he said, pointing at his understudy. "I'm sure Mr. Wolfe's thought about it many times." Grasping James' shoulder, Guy slowly rose to his feet. "You've ruined my career, Victor. All week during dress rehearsals, you've been sitting out there, watching my every move. You planned all this, didn't you? Arrest him, Marshal."

Nora saw Guy clench his fist and pound the air in Victor's direction.

Victor shot out of his seat. "I've done no such thing! You're a liar," he shouted.

Suddenly, the marshal pushed back his chair and climbed down from the stage. Looming over the group, he said, "Enough of this posturing. I'm getting frustrated with all the theatrics. I don't want to call in Sheriff Connery at this stage of the investigation, but I won't hesitate to do so if I need to keep order. "

Hearing the marshal bring up Jimmy Connery's name shocked Nora. As a reporter, it was likely that she would have to speak to Monterey County's newly appointed sheriff at some point. Right now, she wasn't sure where this developing story was going. But she was positive that she would find a future meeting with Jimmy very uncomfortable, given their past history.

Marshal Englund's voice interrupted her thoughts. "I want you to write your names, addresses and telephone numbers on this sheet of paper, so I can contact you later. And remember what I said. Nobody has my permission to leave town."

After complying with his order, Nora took off Randall's jacket and returned it to him. She decided that she would contact Marshal Englund tomorrow, to tell him about the cream pitcher being moved off the serving tray. More than likely, it was just Burt's mistake, but she had to mention it.

A light tap on her shoulder made her turn around.

"I'm sorry I accused you earlier, Nora," Vera said. "I think my words came out wrong. I was so scared when I saw that hole appear in the carpet."

As she reached over to give the actress a hug, Nora detected a spicy, sensual scent. It was most unusual. She said, "No harm done. We're all a bit on edge."

"Thanks for being so understanding. I'm going to help Guy get home now. We both rent rooms at the San Carlos Lodge. Will you be playing softball in the morning?"

"When have you ever known me to miss an Abalone League practice? Or you either, for that matter? I'll see you then."

Smiling, Vera took hold of Guy's outstretched hand. The two of them walked off.

Leaving the theater, Nora spotted Marshal Englund's black

stallion tethered to a pine tree next to the ticket booth. Billy whinnied and bobbed his head when she stopped to pat him on the nose. It pleased her that he remembered her. Too bad she didn't have an apple to give him.

On her way back to the newspaper office, Nora found the business district deserted. Thankfully, no one would stop and gawk at her outlandish costume. She paused to admire the row of bushy pine trees that ran the length of the recently paved main street. They were forming a natural median that would discourage future parking in the center of Ocean Avenue. Carmel was changing, and new buildings were going up. She hoped the Blue Bird Tea Room would remain untouched. Last November, she and Sheriff Jimmy Connery had first met for lunch at the village's popular café. With her having turned down his offer of marriage a month ago, talking to him now would be difficult, if not impossible.

CHAPTER FOUR

Feeling at loose ends, William Owens ambled over to the *Carmel Pine Cone's* front window and stared out at Ocean Avenue. With darkness falling, he wondered if the city fathers would ever agree to install one or two street lights in the downtown business district. Here he was, still at work, ostensibly to repair a malfunctioning printing press, but in fact, he had purposely delayed going home. Closing his eyes, he allowed himself a moment of self-pity.

Thinking back, he recalled his wife's parting words to him at the Monterey train station a week ago: 'I can't see why you didn't try harder to find someone to take over for you, William. I don't know how I'm going to explain your absence to Mother.'

He had understood why her father's death was something that Mary Lee had to attend to, but she didn't understand that he had a duty to publish the village's newspaper every week. He had been doing the job for seven years now, and the effort involved a time commitment that he couldn't shrug off — not even for a funeral. Most years, their vacations consisted of a weekend camping trip in Big Sur, then right back home. Now Mary Lee wanted him to be away from work for three weeks. Well, he couldn't do it.

Standing together on the train's platform, he had kissed her cheek and said, 'You're just upset because your mother will think I'm leading a gay bachelor's life here in Carmel while you're away in Chicago.'

'Mind your speech in front of Sally,' his wife had scolded. Then, taking their daughter's hand, she had boarded the train without looking back.

Dasher's barking interrupted his reverie. Pulling a piece of ham from a stale left-over sandwich, Owens dangled the meat in front of his Welsh corgi. Sprawled near the door, the dog leapt up and caught the morsel lobbed at him. Twirling around, he barked again as the front door opened.

Sidestepping the dog, Nora said, "Down, Dasher!"

"I wasn't expecting you," William said. Her flushed cheeks told him that she was excited about something. "Is your play rehearsal over this early?" he asked.

"It was cancelled. I came back to the office, in hopes of finding you."

Her unexpected appearance boosted his spirits. As he looked at her, it occurred to him that he had never thought of her as an appealing young woman before. Her face and figure reminded him of how his wife had looked when they were first courting.

"Something awful has happened at the theater," Nora said, as she sat down on the bench intended for their customers.

William pulled up a nearby chair. "What's wrong?"

"Our prop man, Burt Erickson, was injured tonight. The doctor was called to examine him. Apparently Burt lost a lot of blood and he probably has a concussion."

"That's terrible. Did he take a fall?"

"No. He claims he was struck from behind by an unknown assailant. But there's more. Besides the attack on him, someone also injured Guy Porter, our leading actor. He drank some milk from my tea service and it seriously burned his throat. Marshal

Englund came to the theater and he's been interviewing the cast for the past hour."

William looked up at the wall clock. "It's late and I don't think we should get into this tonight, Honora. Tomorrow will be soon enough. The Pine Inn's dining room is still serving supper. Let's go over there and get a bite to eat. I'll bet you haven't had anything since lunchtime."

His invitation served to revive Nora. "That sounds good to me," she said. "I hadn't realized it, but actually, I'm starving." Getting up from the bench, she added, "If you'll excuse me, I'm going to change out of this silly outfit and then I'll be ready to join you." Taking off her maid's cap, she headed for the office bathroom.

When she returned minutes later, she said, "I'd like to start working up the story before the Monterey daily paper gets wind of it, Mr. Owens. One of their reporters might write a skewed article questioning the safety of attending plays at the Forest Theater, and we all know what that would do to our attendance. Carmel has to attract much bigger audiences if we want our theater to remain viable."

Listening to her arguments, William suddenly realized that Honora Finnegan was no longer the inexperienced cub reporter he had hired a year ago. She was developing into a very competent journalist.

Shutting off the lights, the two headed down Ocean Avenue and crossed to the other side of the street at Lincoln. They were the last people to be seated in the Pine Inn's comfortable dining room. The waiter took their orders and brought their meals promptly. Nora and William talked about the newspaper business while they ate.

Taking out his change purse, he paid the bill and then looked over at her. "Start writing your article when you get home,

Honora. We'll go over it tomorrow as soon as you come in."

"I'll have it ready for you when I arrive at noon."

Getting up, he helped her into her coat. "Being a single woman and the only daughter of my oldest friend, I always worry about your personal safety. In light of what happened at play rehearsal tonight, coupled with the ongoing rivalry between our two theater companies, the last thing I want is for you to come to any harm by getting mixed up in it."

"I'll be careful," she said, as she bent to light the candle in her small tin lantern.

They walked out the Pine Inn's front door onto Ocean Avenue. William waited until Nora reached the corner of Monte Verde Street, where she waved before continuing on toward home. As he walked back to the office, he mulled over her account of the malicious assaults at the Forest Theater. He knew that the two incidents would instantly trigger a community-wide uproar. He would give the reading public as much information as possible on the criminal investigation that would ensue. The seriousness of the crimes demanded that he publish an extra issue of the paper at the beginning of the week. He would make sure that it was posted on the village's bulletin board. And in the morning, he would send a telegram to his wife in Chicago. Hopefully, when she read his news, Mary Lee would understand why he was right to remain in Carmel.

Reaching the office, he pulled on the string attached to the ceiling light. Dasher barked. "O.K., boy," he said to the corgi. "It's time for us to head home."

Coming through her cottage's back door, Nora pushed off her shoes and dropped her purse on the kitchen table. She turned on the lights and felt grateful once again for her next door neighbor's many acts of kindness. Lucinda Newsom's old wicker basket, which she had left on Nora's porch, contained three fresh eggs and a loaf of the woman's homemade bread. It wasn't the equal of a special supper at the Pine Inn with Mr. Owens, she thought, but a meal of scrambled eggs and toast in the morning would be perfect.

She considered how curious it was to be writing an article about the vicious incidents that had taken place at the theater earlier. What made it harder was that, this time, she was an integral part of the story.

The sound of footsteps on the back stairs startled her. Pushing aside the window curtain over the kitchen sink, Nora peered out at two men who were standing on the porch. One of them was her friend, Keith Preston, Carmel's librarian. He waved at her. She didn't recognize his companion. Going to the door, she opened it part way. "Is something wrong?" she asked. "It's awfully late, Keith."

"I know, Nora, and I should have telephoned. But it's important and kind of an emergency. Let us in before we alarm the neighbors and ruin your reputation."

Grinning, she said, "I'm certain Mrs. Newsom has already seen you. But come in anyway." Opening the door wider, she stood to one side. As they stepped forward, she could see the family resemblance. Both young men had the same wavy blond hair and blue eyes, but the stranger was taller and a bit heavier than Keith.

"Nora, this is my brother, Lee," he said. "He arrived for a visit a few days ago."

"I'm pleased to meet you, Mr. Preston. I've heard so much about you."

"It's my pleasure to meet you," Lee Preston said in a slow, southern drawl. "Keith has told me a lot about you as well. I feel as if I know you."

Nora blushed. What an attractive man, she thought. In contrast to Keith's paint-stained denim shirt and worn trousers, his brother was attired in pressed tan slacks and an open-collared white shirt under a linen jacket. A white silk scarf was tied around his neck. "Come in," she said. "May I offer you a cold drink? I have ginger beer handy."

"Don't you have something a little stronger?" Keith said, as he sidled past her and headed for the kitchen table.

"I see you've forgotten about Prohibition," Nora said.

Frowning at his older brother, Lee turned to leave. "We shouldn't stay, Keith. I told you on the way over here that we would be bothering the young lady."

"Nonsense. Nora knows all the people connected with the play you were watching at the Forest Theater this afternoon. I think she's your best source for advice."

"Now you've piqued my curiosity," Nora said. "Please sit down, both of you." Going over to the icebox, she pulled out three bottles. Removing the caps and getting a water glass for her drink, she said, "Why don't you start by telling me what happened?"

The three settled around the table, and for the next few minutes, Lee shared some disturbing information. When he finished, he said, "What do you think I should do, Nora?"

"You need to contact Marshal Englund, our local policeman. He'll be in his office at City Hall by eight o'clock in the morning."

"Lee doesn't know his way around Carmel," Keith interjected. "And I'm due at the library first thing. I'm hosting a rummage sale to raise extra funds for our children's book collection. Can you go with him, Nora?"

Pushing back his chair, Lee stood up. "It's an imposition, Nora, but I'd be very pleased for the support."

"I'll be happy to," Nora said. "I too have something to share with the marshal, and it's relevant to what you observed at the theater earlier. However, there is a problem. I have softball practice at nine o'clock and it's a very long walk out to Carmel Point."

Lee's face broke into a smile. "I'd be delighted to take you there. I recently bought a new touring car in San Francisco and drove it down here. I'll pick you up a little before eight, and after we both speak to the marshal, I'll escort you to the baseball diamond."

Nora laughed. "Carmel's playing field is best described as a 'diamond in the rough,' I'm afraid. But thank you for offering me a ride."

After seeing the brothers out, Nora sat down at the table to compose her article. She hoped to be able to insert Lee Preston's account of what he had seen on stage at the Forest Theater into her news story. However, she was certain that she would have to clear that first with Carmel's lawman, Marshal Gus Englund.

CHAPTER FIVE

Saturday

The clock on the fireplace mantel reminded Nora that she had time to run an errand before Lee Preston's arrival. She closed her cottage's front door behind her and hurried out to Monte Verde Street. The weather was a typical summer morning in Carmel, with an overcast sky that would burn off by noon. Under her sweater, she wore a white middy blouse and a knee-length pleated skirt, her former tennis outfit that she had pressed into service for playing softball.

A few minutes later, she arrived at the corner milk shrine, where she picked up her pint of milk and left a Buffalo nickel wrapped in paper with her order for tomorrow. As she was about to return home, she decided to check the shelf directly below hers. Cradling a second pint of milk and a packet of butter, she retraced her steps and knocked on her next door neighbor's back door.

"Good morning, Nora," Lucinda Newsom called out as soon as she opened it.

"Good morning." Nora held out the dairy products. "I've brought your order from the shrine. I wanted to save you a trip in this cool weather."

"That's very nice of you, Nora, but I'll miss my daily visit with Mrs. Philbrook."

Nora knew that their elderly neighbor across the street always had some gossipy tidbit to share with Mrs. Newsom around the corner milk shrine. "I'm sorry," she said, "but I had to do a little something extra to thank you for sharing your eggs and that delicious bread. I had them for breakfast."

Attired in a woolen bathrobe and slippers, Mrs. Newsom stepped out on the porch. Taking Nora's arm, she said, "You know, you're not eating properly, and I've been a little concerned about who those men were who came visiting you last night."

Before the woman could begin one of her well-meaning lectures, Nora said, "Thanks again, Mrs. Newsom, but I'd better be going. You see, I have an appointment at City Hall in a few minutes." Stepping off the porch, Nora headed home to put her milk in the icebox and pick up her baseball mitt.

For a second time, she shut her front door and walked out to the road to wait for Keith's younger brother. What was keeping him? It was after eight o'clock.

Within minutes, she heard the sound of a fast approaching vehicle. When it slowed and came to a halt, Nora was sure she had never seen an automobile with such bright, cherry red paint. It was a two-door coupe, but it had both front and rear seats. The elongated front hood sported a prominent temperature gauge and vertical louvers along the sides. Pneumatic tires covered each of the twelve-spoke wooden wheels.

Shutting off the engine, Lee stepped out on the driver's side and came to stand beside Nora. He said, "Sorry I'm late. I changed my clothes at the last minute."

She was surprised to see him so casually dressed in a pullover sweater, gray knickers, tartan patterned stockings and high-top work boots — the kind that engineers wore. She had to admit that he looked quite dashing.

"I'd like to join you and your friends on the softball field later on," he said. "I love the game and I really need the exercise." Opening the passenger door for her, he continued, "Take a look inside and tell me what you think of her."

Nora leaned forward to examine the automobile's interior and instantly caught the distinctive aroma of leather seat covers. "It's luxurious," she said. "I'm impressed." She wondered how a man in his twenties could afford to own such an expensive machine. It was then that she realized she had no idea what Lee Preston did for a living.

He helped her into the passenger seat, closed her door, and went around the front to get in on the driver's side. Resting his hands on the steering wheel, he said, "We're sitting in the latest eight-cylinder Cadillac Victoria. She can go sixty-five miles an hour, but most of the roads between here and San Francisco don't allow that kind of speed."

"It must be wonderful to drive a vehicle like this. Unfortunately, women don't often get the chance to experience it." Nora didn't want to admit that she had asked her father for driving lessons, but he had refused outright. He explained that he expected her future husband to teach her — that is, if he were so inclined.

Placing her baseball mitt on the back seat, she said, "If you don't mind my asking, what are you doing here, Lee? Keith has told me that you graduated from the College of Charleston. What did you study, and do you still live in South Carolina?"

"No, I don't. I majored in literature." Leaning forward in his seat, he began fiddling with a knob on the dashboard. "I'm a true Confederate, Nora. I bought this particular model because it has a cigar lighter right here. You know we Southerners enjoy our tobacco."

Men and their smoking, Nora thought. "You still haven't told me where you live now."

"I always wanted to try my luck at writing, and after reading in the *New York Times* that the Hollywood film studios were looking for screenwriters, I took the train to Los Angeles on a whim. I've been quite successful. I've sold a dozen screenplays, and all of them have been made into motion pictures."

Nora had never met anyone who worked in the film industry. She guessed that Lee had a very lucrative job. "It all sounds so glamorous," she said.

He shook his head. "It's actually pretty hectic." Reaching out, he pressed the electric starter to the engine. "You know, this is the type of automobile that you could learn to drive. It doesn't need to be hand-cranked to start up. While I'm here in Carmel, I'd be happy to give you a few lessons."

Nora wondered if he was being serious, or just flirting. She imagined the freedom she would enjoy if she learned to drive. She would be able to go anywhere she wanted to travel. But she decided not to pursue his offer for now.

After making sure there was no other traffic nearby, Lee swung the Cadillac around and headed for Ocean Avenue and the village's business district.

When he slowed down at the next intersection, Nora said, "I think it's good that you want to spend time with your brother."

"Quite honestly, I hadn't planned on taking this trip. I've been far too busy."

"What changed your mind then?"

"Last week I received a telephone call from Herbert Heron. He invited me to meet with him. So I took the train to San Francisco, purchased this car, and drove here."

"Really? I don't understand, Lee. Why would the founder of the Forest Theater Society want to meet with you? He doesn't even know you."

"That's true, but there is something that I haven't shared with you. I wrote a stage play during my final semester at the College of Charleston. At Keith's urging, I entered it into Carmel's annual play competition last spring."

"But you didn't win first prize. A local playwright, James Carpenter, did. It's his play that I'm acting in."

"I know. But mine received second place honors."

"Then what would prompt Mr. Heron to invite you here?"

He laughed. "You're a very persistent woman, Miss Finnegan. It must be due to your reporter's instincts. Heron would like to put on my play this season. It would be satisfying for me to see and hear a live audience react to what I've written. That isn't possible when one works in the movies."

Nora was dumbfounded. "I can't believe it. From what you've said, Mr. Heron is going to cancel the Western Drama Society's play, even though the Board that runs the Forest Theater Society has already awarded the prize money to James Carpenter."

"I don't know anything about that. Yesterday Mr. Heron told me that Carpenter went against longstanding Carmel tradition and brought in an actor named Guy Porter. Not only is this fellow an outsider, but a professionally trained actor as well."

"You're correct. And Perry Newberry, another prominent member of the Board, has voiced his strong opposition in a letter he's written to my newspaper."

"I was asked to keep all this information confidential, Nora. I hope you'll honor Mr. Heron's request."

Nora nodded, but she remained confused. "Our play has one final dress rehearsal and then we're opening next week. With two plays already in production, and only a single theater available for performances, I don't see how yours can be scheduled."

"That may change."

As she listened to him, Nora wondered if Lee had come to stay. She knew it would be difficult for him to drive his new automobile back to Southern California. Many of the county roads between Carmel and Hollywood were basically unimproved.

Looking out the front window, she saw that they had come to the intersection of Ocean Avenue. "You have to go right here," she said. Pointing across the street, she continued, "That's the Pine Inn, our oldest and finest hotel. It's been expanded, of course, but some years ago, the original building was rolled down to this new site from the upper end of Ocean Avenue."

"That must have been quite a feat. I have a nice room there on the second floor with a fantastic ocean view."

"Aren't you staying with your brother?"

Lee chuckled. "Keith's cabin has only a single bed." He winked and added, "I'm far too old to sleep on the floor."

Turning the corner, they headed uphill towards Dolores Street.

"City Hall is there on the left," Nora said.

After Nora introduced Lee to Marshal Gus Englund, he escorted them to his first floor office at the rear of City Hall. Above it was the upstairs meeting room where Carmel's elected officials regularly met. In her job as a reporter for the *Pine Cone* this past year, she had spent many hours in that second floor chamber.

Pointing to two chairs, Englund said, "I'll be right back with some fresh coffee."

Seated next to Lee in front of the marshal's uncluttered oak desk, Nora looked around and said, "I was here last November, and from what I can see, nothing much has changed."

Lee was staring at the only piece of wall decoration — a framed copy of the U. S. Constitution. "This room would make a very attractive set for a cowboy movie," he said. "It's pretty stark."

When the marshal returned, he set three steaming mugs of coffee on the desk. Going behind it, he sat down and reached into the bottom drawer. Bringing out a tin box, he looked at Nora.

"Have some of Mrs. Englund's gingersnaps. I remember how much you liked them the last time you were here, Miss Finnegan. Now tell me, is today's visit newspaper business?"

Lee piped up. "I'm afraid this is all my doing, Marshal. Miss Finnegan thinks I witnessed something at the theater yesterday that is relevant to your investigation. Let me start at the beginning. I arrived in Carmel a few days ago at Herbert Heron's invitation. I'm staying at the Pine Inn. Yesterday I telephoned Mr. Heron and we arranged to meet at the Forest Theater. A young man named Tommy, who was sweeping the stage, pointed out Mr. Heron to me. I went over to speak with him while Tommy put up the set for one of the plays. When Heron and I finished our discussion, I decided to take a seat in the last row of the theater and wait for the rehearsal of Mr. Carpenter's play to begin. That's when I noticed another man come out on stage. He was carrying a rather small pitcher."

"Did you recognize him?" Englund asked.

Lee shook his head. "No, sir, I didn't. I watched him go to the edge of the stage and fill the pitcher with water from a hose. He took a drink from it; then he poured out the remaining water and went back stage."

"So at that point in time the pitcher was completely empty," Englund said.

Lee nodded. "I didn't think anything of it until later, while I was listening to you interrogate the cast. That's when I realized that I had seen something important. So I discussed the matter with my brother and Miss Finnegan."

Englund frowned. "You ought to have come forward last night and told me about what you'd seen."

"I know I should have, but as a stranger, I didn't want to get involved. I'm sorry that I didn't."

Putting down her coffee mug, Nora said, "I have a confession too, Marshal. I ought to have shared something with you that happened to me as well. I arrived late at the theater yesterday and I found the cream pitcher to my tea set sitting off to one side of the other items on the tray. It wasn't where our prop man, Burt Erickson, usually puts it."

"Was it empty?"

"No. It had some milk in it. At least I thought it was milk. Normally, it would be empty, but since this was a full dress rehearsal, the director told Burt to put milk in it this time."

Englund rubbed his chin. "It seems that whoever added the corrosive substance to the milk didn't put the pitcher on your tea tray, Nora."

"I agree, Marshal. Is there a way to find out what that substance was?"

Englund nodded. "Last night I stopped by the drug store and gave it to our pharmacist, Doc Staniford. He's doing an analysis of what was left in the pitcher." Looking over at Lee, he continued, "Mr. Preston, I need you to give me the name of the man you saw carrying the cream pitcher last night."

Hesitating and looking down at his folded hands, Lee didn't respond.

"I ask you again, young man. Who did you see? I want an answer."

Squaring his shoulders, Lee looked at the marshal. "I hope I'm not going to be responsible for getting an innocent man in trouble. I didn't know him, but after describing him to Miss Finnegan last night, I do now. It was Guy Porter's understudy, Victor Wolfe."

CHAPTER SIX

After meeting with Marshal Englund at City Hall, Nora and Lee left the business district and traveled south. At times Lee had to maneuver the touring car around a pine or oak tree that was growing in the center of one of Carmel's many unpaved streets.

"I'd have to say that driving here is a challenge," Lee said.

Nora shrugged. "It's just that we don't want to disturb any of our trees, so we make people go around them."

About a half-mile past Thirteenth Avenue, they arrived at a headland covered with windswept grasses. The cries of passing seabirds overhead intermingled with the rushing sounds of the waves crashing on the beach below.

"What a beautiful view," Lee said, as he pulled over to the side of the road.

Nora settled back in her seat. "It's odd, but whenever I visit Carmel Point, I always feel a sense of calm come over me. It's something that I never experience anywhere else."

"I have the same feeling when I'm standing on the Battery in Charleston and staring across the water at Fort Sumter. Given this area's natural beauty, I'm really surprised that more people don't live out this way. So far, we've come across only one or two houses."

"Those who settle here have to give up certain amenities," Nora said, as she pointed at a pair of prominent stone structures standing close together on a low hillock near the shoreline.

"That's the home of our resident poet, Robinson Jeffers and his wife Una. They don't mind that electricity doesn't come out this far. That tower you see going up next to their cottage is going to be his private retreat. He's building it himself by moving stones up from the cove below."

"He must be a very talented person," Lee mused. "As a fellow writer, I can understand why Mr. Jeffers would value this isolation."

Noise from a crowd off in the distance caught Nora's attention. "We'd better be going, or else morning practice will have started."

Lee put the Cadillac in gear and drove to an area where a dozen automobiles, all of them empty, were sitting in a semicircle around a large clearing. Parking nearby, he reached into the back seat and handed Nora her baseball mitt. Getting out of the vehicle, they walked toward a cleared dirt area where a young man was busy chalking the diamond's first and third base lines.

"Now I see what you meant by a 'diamond in the rough,'" Lee kidded.

Nora laughed. "That fellow working on the field is a friend of mine by the name of Rob Jacklin. He teaches fourth grade at Sunset School and supervises the Boys Club. On weekends, he always prepares the baseball diamond for our games."

"He certainly can draw a straight line. But what are those boys over there doing with rolled-up newspapers?"

"They're stuffing all the gopher holes."

Lee looked shocked. "Whatever for?"

"We want to avoid injuries. No one needs an ankle sprain or a broken leg while playing. But if someone does suffer one, our village druggist, Doc Staniford, is here to deal with it. He brings a supply of bandages, splints and crutches to every game."

As she looked around at the various men, women and children who were engaged in throwing and catching softballs, Nora realized that two of her fellow "Cardinals" were missing. Claudia Jacklin, Rob's wife and the female lead in Nora's play, was absent, as was Vera Winfield, Claudia's understudy. Both women had specifically told her that they would see her this morning at softball practice.

"Wait here," she said to Lee. "I'm going over to speak to Rob. I'll be back in a minute."

Wearing a pair of old dungarees and a long-sleeved navy sweater with "Blue Jays" embroidered across the front, Rob Jacklin stopped what he was doing when he saw Nora. His angular features and lean frame always reminded her of an heroic figure in one of her childhood adventure books.

Standing up and brushing his hair out of his eyes, he grinned. "It's good to see you, Nora. Who's the handsome stranger who brought you in that flashy red Cadillac?"

"That's Lee Preston, Keith's younger brother. He arrived from Hollywood a few days ago."

"Hollywood, eh? Maybe he'll convince one of the film studios down there to give you a screen test? You're certainly pretty enough."

Nora's face reddened. "Thanks, but I could never compete with Mary Pickford, nor you with Douglas Fairbanks, for that matter."

Like her, Rob always enjoyed their easy banter. Looking over at Lee, he said, "Seriously, it would be good for you to have a new admirer. You've been awfully moody since you and Jimmy parted ways. I hope Lee plans on staying a while."

"I don't need another beau. I'm concentrating on my career. You know that. Where's Claudia? I hope her absence doesn't mean that Freddie is still under the weather."

"Unfortunately, his fever hasn't gone down much and she's been tending him since yesterday. Doctor Barnes came to the house after supper last night and took a look at Freddie. He recommended aspirin, cool sponge baths and lots of liquids until his fever breaks. It's difficult keeping the boy down. He begged us to let him come to practice."

"I hope he's better soon. By the way, where is Vera? Did you stop by for her?"

"I did, but she wasn't out front of the lodge as she always is. I thought she had found a ride with someone else. Since I was late, I left, after waiting a few minutes."

"That's puzzling. Vera left the theater with Guy Porter last night. I wonder what happened? Without her and Claudia, our softball team won't have enough players."

"We can always put together a pick-up team."

"It's probably nothing, but I think I'll go back to Vera's place. Tell Claudia hello for me and that I'll call her later."

Walking over to Lee, who was limbering up by swinging a bat back and forth, Nora said, "I know you've been looking forward to some exercise this morning, but I have an errand to run. Would you be willing to drive me?"

Lee dropped the bat. "I'm at your beck and call. Where are we headed?"

"The place I need to go to is near Sunset School."

Bumping their way back to town along uneven dirt roads, they reached Ninth Avenue. Nora said, "That's the San Carlos Lodge over there."

Lee slowed down, made a wide U-turn on San Carlos Street, and parked in front of a large, two-story Craftsman-style residence, its walls faced with random-patterned field stones. "It's quite an impressive structure," he said.

"Yes, it is. I've always liked this building. Originally, it was a family home. Now it's a rooming house for people who work in the business district. It's an easy walk to the retail shops and art galleries along Ocean Avenue."

Nora knew from having visited Vera here that the lodge provided long-term accomodations to some half a dozen Carmelites. Though the rooms were spartan, the lodge's proprietor, Annie Stevens, included breakfast and dinner for ten dollars a month. Annie treated all her boarders as family and knew pretty much what was going on in their daily lives. So it didn't surprise Nora when she and Lee walked into Annie's kitchen to find out from the short, middle-aged woman that Vera had been up all night, caring for a seriously ill Guy.

"The poor girl's in no condition to be playing softball with you this morning, Nora," Annie said. "She's been keeping watch over Guy, praying and worrying about him. Now don't take this wrong, dear. I never allow an unmarried couple to share the same room. However, after seeing how bad he was last night, I made an exception to my policy. I imagine Vera's been in and out of Guy's room all night."

"How is he feeling now?"

Shaking her head, Annie's eyes teared up. "Last night, he wasn't breathing too well. I told Vera that I thought we had better have Doctor Barnes take a look at him. He came here about four o'clock this morning. And apparently, the doctor helped Guy quite a bit. I was just about to go check on him and offer him and Vera some breakfast. Since they're my only boarders at the moment, how about I fix you two some pancakes while I'm at it?"

"That's very nice of you, but I've had my breakfast," Nora said.

"Nothing for me either," Lee said, "but thank you anyway."

"If it's all right," Nora said, "I'd like to go up and see Vera and ask her about Guy. From what you've told us, it sounds like he's gotten worse since Doctor Barnes first treated him at the theater last night. What room is he staying in?"

"As you know from your past visits, Nora, I've given my rooms names, not numbers. Vera's staying in the Cypress and Guy is across the way in the Oaks."

"Would you allow Mr. Preston to come up with me? I might need his help if Guy should ask to be taken to the doctor's office."

Annie looked Lee up and down. "You look decent enough to me, young man. You can go with her."

At the top of the stairs, Nora and Lee paused at the landing. Ahead of them was a a corridor covered with oak plank flooring running the length of the second floor. The high pitched ceiling with exposed rafters, from which dangled several electric cords with light bulbs, kept the narrow passageway from feeling oppressive. All the doors along the hallway had the names of trees painted in gold letters on the overhead frames. On both sides, the walls were covered with framed paintings of varying sizes.

"Some of these art works have price tags on them," Lee noted.

"That's right. Annie once told me that the artists who rent rooms from her use this hall as a sales gallery. It's their way of paying her for their room and board. Most of the paintings are plein-air works of the coastline and Big Sur."

Examining a small oil painting of Carmel Point, Lee said, "This is better than a photograph."

Halfway down the hall, they spotted two doors side-by-side with partially-opened glass transoms above them. One door was marked "M," the other "F."

"It sounds like water's running in there," Nora said, as she and Lee passed the women's bathroom.

From inside, a voice shouted, "Nora, is that you? Who are you talking to?"

"Vera, are you in there?"

"I've just had a bath. Come on in. I'm dressed."

Lee stepped back. "I'll wait here."

Nora opened the door and entered the bathroom, its floor covered with small white tiles in a chicken wire pattern. A claw foot tub occupied the far wall. A toilet with an overhead water tank and a large pedestal sink were opposite. Vera was combing her hair in front of the mirror and asked, "Who's out there?"

"You don't know him. Keith Preston's brother is in town for a visit. He drove me here. I was worried when you didn't come to softball practice. I decided I'd better check on you and Guy."

Stepping away from the sink, Vera said, "It's been terrible, Nora. Guy got so bad during the night that Annie made me call the doctor. He was just heading out to deliver a baby, but he came right over. He did something drastic to help Guy breathe better, since his throat was nearly closed off."

"What did he do?"

"I don't know exactly because he asked me to step out of the room. When he came out, Doctor Barnes said that Guy was breathing much better and had dropped off to sleep. The doctor had to get back to the pregnant woman and said he would come back later if needed. I felt relieved and went to bed."

"Let's go see how Guy's doing," Nora said. "Also, I'd like you to meet Lee." Opening the bathroom door, Nora stepped out.

"Lee, this is Vera Winfield, a friend of Guy Porter's."

"Nice to meet you, Mr. Preston," Vera said.

"The pleasure's mine," Lee replied.

"Guy's room is the last one on the left," Vera said, as she knocked on the door. "Guy? Are you awake? You have some visitors." Opening the door, and looking in, Vera cried out, "Oh my God!"

Nora pushed past her and sidestepped a pile of rumpled bedding strewn across the floor. Between it and the bed lay Guy's contorted body, his face blue, his knees drawn up, his left hand clutching his throat. The actor's eyes were wide open, but lifeless.

Lee knelt down to feel Guy's neck for a pulse.

That was when Nora noticed something on the carpet under the bed: a silver tube that curved like one of her father's fish hooks. It lay a few inches away from Guy's right hand.

Vera, who had remained at the door, wailed, "He's dead, isn't he?"

CHAPTER SEVEN

The cuckoo clock in the lodge's front parlor struck ten, as Nora, Lee and Vera came downstairs. They found Annie Stevens setting the breakfast table in her sun-filled kitchen. "Whatever's the matter?" she said. "Is Guy feeling worse?"

Nora took her hand. "I'm afraid we have some bad news. Guy's not breathing."

Reaching for the back of a chair, Annie steadied herself. "You mean he's dead?"

"We think so, but we should call Doctor Barnes right away," Nora said.

Face ashen, Annie pressed her hand to her chest. "The telephone's over there by the back door. Call him, will you, Nora? I can't think straight."

Nora went to the telephone and called.

Going over to Vera, Annie opened her arms and hugged her. The two women clung to one another. "I'm so sorry, dear," Annie said. "I know how much Guy means to you. You've fallen in love with him right under my nose."

Vera began sobbing uncontrollably. Lee pulled out a clean handkerchief from his pocket and pressed it into her hands.

Nora hung up the telephone and said, "The doctor will be

right over. He said we shouldn't disturb anything in Guy's room. He's calling Marshal Englund."

"Let's move into the dining room," Annie said. "We'll be more comfortable."

Ten minutes later, Nora, Lee, Annie and Vera were seated at the table, cups of tea in front of them, when they heard a knock on the lodge's front door.

"That's Doctor Barnes," Annie said. "He'll let himself in, just like he did earlier this morning. He knows I never lock my doors." Sniffling, she added, "If I did, I'd never get any sleep. My roomers come and go at all hours of the day and night."

Carrying his black leather bag through the archway into the dining room, Doctor Zachary Barnes waved at Annie. He had taken over another physician's medical practice a couple of months ago. Nora had seen him once or twice while making a purchase at Levy's general store. Tall, clean-shaven, and wearing a black suit, white shirt and tie, his youthful face showed no evidence of urgency or anxiety. Instead, it displayed a friendly, calm demeanor. She liked him immediately.

Without waiting for introductions from Annie, the doctor said, "I have to tell you, Mrs. Stevens, that I'm very puzzled about Mr. Porter. When I left him this morning, he was doing so much better. I'll go up now." With that, he retraced his steps and hurried up the front hall stairs.

Moments later, a loud knock on the front door signaled the arrival of Marshal Gus Englund. When he walked into the room, Annie spoke up. "Mr. Porter's bedroom is upstairs at the end of the hall, Marshal. You'll find the doctor there."

After about fifteen minutes, which seemed like an eternity to Nora, the two men returned to the group waiting for them in the dining room. The doctor took a seat at one end of the table and the marshal sat at the other end.

Marshal Englund spoke first. "I'm ruling Mr. Porter's death as murder."

Vera gasped and began to cry. Sitting next to her, Annie put her arm around the young woman's shoulders and tried to comfort her.

"I'm going to contact the county sheriff, who will take over the investigation I've begun," the marshal said. "There will be a coroner's autopsy." Looking at Nora, he continued, "Since Miss Finnegan from the *Pine Cone* is present and will be reporting the news of Mr. Porter's death, I want the public to know how he died. I'm going to ask Doctor Barnes to tell all of you what he told me upstairs."

Nora reached for her purse and pulled out her notebook and pencil.

Clearing his throat, the doctor began, "Thank you, Marshal. Mr. Porter expired because he was unable to breathe due to the swelling in his throat. He had ingested a corrosive liquid yesterday and got much worse during the night. When I saw him a few hours ago, he could hardly catch his breath. I did a tracheotomy. I inserted a tube into his windpipe to bypass the swollen throat. It was subsequently removed and he died because he couldn't breathe."

Nora interrupted, "I noticed a curved, blood-stained, silver tube lying on the floor next to Guy. Is that what you're referring to, Doctor Barnes?"

He nodded. "Yes, Miss Finnegan, Marshal Englund found it there. I had it firmly secured with a strong cloth tape that I knotted at the back of Mr. Porter's neck."

"Could the tube have accidentally fallen out?" she asked.

"I've never heard of any case where a tube has accidentally extruded itself from a patient. That's based on my experience and extensive training with Doctor Chevalier Jackson, a noted laryngologist at Jefferson Medical School in Pennsylvania."

"How rare is this procedure?" Nora probed.

The doctor smiled. "Bypassing the upper airway was done in ancient Egypt. However, during my residency, I placed many of these tubes in adults who had swallowed caustic substances, as well as children who had diphtheria and trouble breathing because of swollen throats."

Englund leaned back in his chair. "From my observation upstairs, I think Mr. Porter had an unwelcome visitor after you left the lodge, Doctor. The tape that was anchoring the tube you put in looks to have been cut. The victim's bedroom was disturbed and he's lying on the floor. I also saw what appear to be scratches on his face and neck, which leads me to think that there was some kind of altercation."

"That can only mean that the tube was forcibly removed," Doctor Barnes added.

"I agree," the marshal said. "It's clear that Mr. Porter died at the hands of another. And there's one more thing. This morning I stopped in to see Doc Staniford at his drugstore. He told me he had analyzed the liquid that Mr. Porter accidentally drank. It had a very corrosive substance called muriatic acid in it."

"That explains the gradual swelling in Mr. Porter's throat and the closing off of his breathing," Doctor Barnes observed.

A teary-eyed Vera raised her hand. "I don't understand. Why didn't Guy call for help? My room is right down the hall from his, and I'm sure I would have heard him."

Shaking his head, the doctor looked at Vera. "Let me explain that to you, young lady. Patients who are intubated can't speak. Air from their lungs that normally activates the vocal chords is funneled out the tube. A patient has to close off the tube opening to make sounds. Mr. Porter probably was fending off his killer and couldn't."

"That's horrible," Vera said. "I can't imagine anything

worse than not being able to speak."

"Is your bedroom upstairs, Mrs. Stevens?" Englund asked.

"No, Marshal, it's downstairs."

"Did you hear any unusual noises during the early morning hours?"

Annie shook her head. "After Doctor Barnes left about four-thirty, I shut off the lights, went back to bed and fell asleep right away. I didn't hear a thing. I woke up an hour ago, when I heard the water running upstairs. I guessed that Vera was taking a bath."

"That would mean that the murder took place sometime between four-thirty and nine," Englund said. "How about you, Miss Winfield? Did you hear anything?"

Wiping her wet eyes with Lee's handkerchief, Vera said, "No, I didn't. I woke up earlier than Annie did. I decided to wait before going in to see Guy. I wanted him to get as much sleep as he could. I took a bath and got dressed. Then Nora and Mr. Preston found me in the bathroom."

Marshal Englund turned to Nora and Lee. "What time did you folks arrive?"

"About nine-thirty," Nora said. "Lee drove me here from Carmel Point." Putting down her pencil, she added, "We came here to see why Vera wasn't at softball practice."

Englund looked at Lee. "Being that you're a playwright, Mr. Preston, I'd like to know if you had any prior contact with Mr. Porter before coming here."

Lee hesitated. Finally, he said, "Yes, I met him, but only once. I was visiting San Francisco this past April. I had been invited to attend a gathering at the Bohemian Grove. Guy and I sat together and we talked about live theater and the movie business."

Englund got up from the table. "All right, that's it for now. I'm going to speak to the doctor in private for a few minutes. Then I want to borrow your telephone, Mrs. Stevens. I need to call Sheriff Connery. I don't want anyone to go into Porter's room."

Vera stood up suddenly and hurried into the kitchen.

"By the way, Mr. Preston, I want you to let me know if you decide to leave town," the marshal said. "I might have some more questions for you."

When Vera returned to the dining room, she approached Nora and Lee, who were preparing to leave. "I just telephoned our director, Nora," Vera said. "I thought James should learn of Guy's death right away. He was devastated by the terrible news, of course, but he intends to hold rehearsal tonight. He told me that Guy would have wanted it that way. He's going to call Victor and ask him to step into Guy's part. Apparently Claudia also telephoned James this morning and said she couldn't make rehearsal because of her son's illness. James wants me to take her role as I did yesterday. Isn't that exciting news?"

Nora was stunned by Vera's quick recovery from her shock at Guy's passing. She said, "Why not take a few days off from your job at the general store and allow yourself time to grieve Guy's loss? I'm sure Mr. Levy will agree."

Vera stepped back. "Acting in James Carpenter's play is what I need now, not grieving. Guy would understand. He'd want me to go on with my acting career." Walking away, she added, "I'll see you at the theater tonight." She ran up the stairs to her bedroom.

Vera's sharp response caused Nora to question the woman's integrity. Was she sincerely interested in Guy or simply playing up to him, as Claudia had suggested to Nora on the telephone yesterday?

As she and Lee walked down the front steps of the lodge, Nora decided to seek a man's opinion. She said, "I'm not really sure what kind of relationship Vera and Guy had. From what you've observed, what do you think?"

Lee shrugged. "Perhaps she wanted to be close to someone who was a celebrity in the theater. After all, Guy was a prominent actor in San Francisco. That kind of needy relationship exists between men and women, Nora. I've seen it in the movie world."

"I guess you're right, but I need to change and get to the newspaper office by noon. I also want to tell Mr. Owens about Guy's murder. Would you drive me home, please?"

"Of course, but let's talk more about relationships tonight. My brother and I are having dinner at my hotel at eight o'clock. Will you join us? What do you say?"

Nora was interested. "All right. I'll meet you at the Pine Inn, but only on one condition."

"And what would that be?"

"That you tell me what you didn't tell the marshal about your meeting with Guy Porter at the Bohemian Grove."

Lee grinned. "I'm not sure you want to know the sordid details, Nora Finnegan."

"Yes, I would. I'm still a reporter."

They headed out to San Carlos Street where Lee's Cadillac was parked.

CHAPTER EIGHT

Carmel village was abuzz. It amazed Nora how quickly the news of Guy Porter's death had spread throughout the business district. Between noon and one o'clock, as she and Mr. Owens made the rounds and picked up the merchants' advertising copy, several residents stopped them and expressed shock at the actor's demise. One man speculated that Porter, an outsider, had been attacked because he didn't belong here. Nora had to admit that she had similar thoughts, but she never envisioned anyone resorting to murder.

When they arrived at the drug store, Owens went off to speak to the pharmacist. Meanwhile, Nora browsed the selection of face creams and powders. She was interrupted by a neighbor whom she had seen yesterday at the corner milk shrine.

"I heard all about the murder this morning, Nora," the woman said. "My friend Betty works at City Hall and she called to tell me about it. She said the young fellow was poisoned and this is going to hurt Annie Steven's boarding house business."

Nora frowned. "To be fair, Ingrid, I don't think you should be spreading gossip. I know for a fact that Annie had no part in what happened to Mr. Porter."

With that, Ingrid rolled her eyes and walked away.

Nora glanced over at Mr. Owens, who was talking with Doc Staniford in front of one of the glass display cabinets. She would have liked to question the druggist about the muriatic acid that someone had added to the milk that Guy drank. She decided to come back later when he was less busy.

Their last stop was the grocery store. Filled with shoppers, Leidig Brothers stocked a variety of canned goods, paper products, and the freshest fruits and vegetables in the area. Customers crowded around the checkout counter, where two clerks scurried back and forth, picking out grocery items from shelves and stacking them on the counter. Before packing them up in brown paper bags, the clerks itemized the prices in pencil on the sides of each bag. Nora marveled at their ability to add them up so quickly. On an easel-like frame to her right rested a blackboard that advertised the store's daily special. While she appreciated a bargain, Nora had no need for a tin of Monterey sardines for ten cents.

Also written on the blackboard was the local weather report, which she knew was taken from the World Almanac. She smiled at today's prediction. The chalked message hadn't been erased for the past month. *Fog clears by mid-day. Rolls back in again by evening. More of the same tomorrow.*

However, a new announcement had been added beneath the weather report: *Walter and Ivy Basham, new owners of the Bath House at foot of Ocean Avenue, invite you to a picnic Sunday afternoon beginning at Two. Free hot dogs.* IF YOU CAN'T GO, WHY NOT TAKE HOME SOME OF LEIDIG'S FINEST HOT DOGS TODAY?

Just then, Owens motioned to her. "Nora," he said, "Mr. Leidig picked up a shipment of fresh strawberries at the Monterey train station early this morning. He wants to advertise them in our next issue. They have to be sold before they spoil. He promised to take out a bigger than usual ad this week. I'll need you to write something that appeals to our women readers and entices them to buy the berries."

Nora nodded. "I'll think of something." She was anxious to start working on her article concerning Guy's murder, not some strawberry story, but she knew how much the *Pine Cone* depended on advertisements. She walked over to the produce section to find inspiration. Looking down, she studied the pile of plump, red strawberries in the cardboard box on the floor. She knew that the darker ones were the sweetest. Reaching for a berry, she pulled off the stem and ate it, allowing its sugary essence to fill her mouth.

Suddenly, an idea popped into her head. She would ask her next door neighbor for permission to publish her traditional strawberry shortcake recipe that had been in Lucinda Newsom's family for several generations. Problem solved.

Returning to the front, she noticed that Mr. Owens was conversing with two of the Leidig brothers. Waving at them, she left the grocery store and returned to the newspaper office. She had a great deal of writing to do this afternoon.

Several hours later, Nora retraced her steps along Ocean Avenue to the drugstore. Entering, she heard the familiar tinkle of the shopkeeper's bell and the whirring of the ceiling fan overhead. Fortunately, the store was empty of customers.

Hearing the bell, Doc Staniford called out, "Good afternoon. Be right with you."

"It's Nora Finnegan, Doc," she called back. "Take your time."

"I promise you'll have my full attention shortly, Nora," he said.

He was probably compounding a patient's prescription, she thought, as she looked around. Having vacationed in Carmel with her parents throughout her childhood, she was still impressed at seeing the many wood drawers stacked halfway up the pharmacy's interior walls that she now knew held customers' files and prescriptions. Above the drawers were rows of shelves with glass doors, behind which she could see dozens of medicine bottles filled with plant extracts and inorganic ingredients. She recalled that mood-altering medicinal herbals and potent analgesics were kept under lock and key in the druggist's private work area at the rear of the store.

Within a few minutes, the pharmacist removed his white apron, placed it on a chair, and came out from behind the back counter. Tall, gray-haired, and in his early fifties, he pushed open the front door to let in some fresh air, and walked over to a bench reserved for waiting customers.

"Is this a good time to talk?" Nora asked.

Nodding, he said, "Let's sit a spell. I've been on my feet ever since I opened at eight o'clock this morning." Removing his wire-rimmed glasses, he pinched his nose and rolled his shoulders.

Nora thought his eyes looked tired. Walking over to sit next to him, she said, "You must have heard that Guy Porter died this morning. I'm writing an article for the paper about it. Marshal Englund told me that you analyzed the substance that Guy accidentally drank at rehearsal last night. He also said that you found muriatic acid mixed in with the milk."

The pharmacist leaned back against the wall, stretched out his legs, and crossed them at the ankles. "It's all very tragic. Chemically speaking, muriatic acid is hydrochloric acid. We humans have a mild form of it in our stomachs."

"Yes. I learned about it in science class during my freshman year at Mills College. The professor called it gastric juice. He said it helps our digestion."

"He was right, but this particular sample was a very concentrated solution of the acid, one that's toxic and corrosive. It causes severe burning of the tissues if swallowed."

"May I quote you on that?"

"By all means."

"What purpose does it have?"

"It's employed as a cleaning agent, like for old bricks that are going to be used again."

"Do you sell muriatic acid here in the drug store?"

Staniford shook his head. "No, I don't. You'd have to go to the lumber yard for that."

"Thank you, Doc. You've been very helpful." Looking up at the clock on the drug store's back wall, Nora realized that play rehearsal would start in the next hour. She stood up. "I won't keep you. You've had a long day."

"It's always good to see you, Nora. Please remember me to your parents."

When she walked out on the Forest Theater's stage at five-thirty that evening, Nora was surprised by the cast's upbeat demeanor. No one appeared to miss their lead actor. His understudy, Victor Wolfe, was sitting in Guy's regular place on the sofa facing the audience. Until tonight, he had never performed in the starring role of James Carpenter's prizewinning play. Seated in an adjacent armchair, Randall King was in the process of lighting his pipe. Nora would soon find out whether his laudatory opinion yesterday regarding Victor's acting skills was warranted.

Claudia Jacklin, ordinarily playing the role of the lead actress, was absent again. Replacing her was a radiant Vera Winfield, who flounced across the stage and took the chair opposite Randall. Leaning forward, she blew a kiss to James Carpenter in the front row. The stagehand, Tommy Anderson, who was carrying some kindling, walked past the director, on his way to the closest fire pit.

James got up and came to the edge of the stage. Looking up

at Nora, he said, "In light of Guy's passing, I've decided to cut out the tea service scene, so as to not remind the audience of what happened here."

Nora sighed. She said, "Although I've been looking forward to being in your play, James, I understand." Inwardly, she had to admit she was disappointed.

Without answering her, he shouted, "All right, people, let's start with Act One."

As Nora left the stage, she heard loud male voices coming from the direction of the theater's entrance. A moment later, three uniformed men strode down the front aisle past a startled Tommy. Nora recognized Marshal Gus Englund leading Sheriff Jimmy Connery and his senior deputy, Alvin Jensen.

Turning to face the intruders, James yelled, "What's the meaning of this, Marshal? You men are disturbing rehearsal. I won't allow it."

"I'm sorry, but it can't be helped, Mr. Carpenter," Englund shot back.

Nora saw Deputy Jensen climb up on the stage and confront Victor. The young man had risen from the sofa, a look of bewilderment on his face.

"You need to come with us, Mr. Wolfe," the deputy said.

Vera too had stood up. "What about our rehearsal? Can these men barge in here like this, James?"

"Everyone, remain in your places," Sheriff Connery said. "We're here to take Mr. Wolfe in for questioning. If that cancels your rehearsal, so be it."

Although uncomfortable at having refused his marriage proposal at the 4th of July picnic, Nora was determined to speak to Jimmy Connery about Guy Porter's murder. She had hurt him deeply, yet the look on his face as she came up to him told her that he still cared. The glowing light from the theater's fire pits made his blue eyes sparkle.

"Hello, Jimmy," she said in a soft voice. "Could I have a few words with you?"

When he didn't answer, she said, "I've been thinking about your daughter Molly lately. She must be getting excited about starting first grade in a few weeks."

When he finally spoke, Jimmy's voice sounded distant and cold. "All you need to know for your newspaper, Miss Finnegan, is that I came to interview a suspect in Mr. Porter's murder. Now please step out of my way."

CHAPTER NINE

On her walk home from the theater, Nora couldn't stop thinking about her embarrassing encounter with Sheriff Jimmy Connery. His abrupt dismissal of her in front of her fellow cast members had been spiteful. It also demonstrated his lack of good manners. What could she expect from a man who dealt with criminals all the time?

Still upset, she arrived at the corner of Ocean Avenue and turned south to her cottage on Monte Verde Street. On the long days of summer, like this one, her next door neighbor, Lucinda Newsom, sat outdoors after supper, in hopes of gossiping with all passersby, as well as catching the nightly breeze coming up from the ocean. Stepping onto the dirt path between their cottages, she found the Newsom porch unoccupied. Luck was with her. She was in no mood to exchange pleasantries with her sweet, but nosy neighbor.

Nora pushed open Pine Log's Dutch door and quietly shut it behind her. She needed to calm down. Stepping into the bathroom, she opened a metal closet and lit the two kerosene burners under the closet's water coils. While waiting for the water to heat up, she changed out of her work clothes in the bedroom and draped her chenille robe over her shoulders. Not only had she been rebuffed by Jimmy, but tonight she had to accept the fact that her acting career was over even before it began. Back in the bathroom, she turned on the bathtub's faucets and filled the tub. Minutes later, she slipped into the hot, steaming water to relax and soothe her upsetting emotions.

Despite Nora's best rationalizations, angry thoughts about Jimmy persisted. It had been difficult to turn down his offer of marriage, but over the past month, and after many sleepless nights, she had succeeded in closing off her fond feelings for him. She had made the decision that her journalist's career was a higher priority for now.

Informing her parents wasn't as difficult as she thought it would be.

'Come home, Nora, dear,' her mother had said. 'We'll find you a suitable beau.'

'I support you completely. You're too good for him,' her father had added.

Finished bathing, Nora donned her robe and walked back to her bedroom. She fully intended to pursue "the sordid details" Lee Preston had yet to divulge about his earlier encounter with Guy Porter at the Bohemian Club. However, she would appear more casual and friendly than businesslike. Her outfit would set the tone. Standing in front of the closet, she examined the clothing she had brought from San Francisco last year. The suits she wore daily to her job at the *Pine Cone* were the first to be eliminated from consideration. They were too practical. She picked out three summery cotton dresses, placed them side by side on the bed and, within moments, rejected each one. They were too flighty.

Returning to the closet, she spotted a two-piece ensemble that her mother had bought for her at the City of Paris. It was definitely something to be worn in San Francisco, but not in Carmel-By-The-Sea. *Except tonight.* Pulling the dress off the hanger, she shook off her robe and slipped the loose-fitting jersey garment over her head. The dropped waist and scalloped handkerchief hemline dipping low in the back flattered her figure. The soft mauve color did wonders for her blue eyes and dark hair. She added the second piece, a straight-cut long-sleeved jacket of the same jersey fabric with a collar designed to hang like a scarf when left untied. Grateful that the era of stiff corsets was over, she studied herself in the mirror. She felt energized. Sitting on the edge of the bed, she put on silk stockings and pumps. She hadn't quite decided whether to wear the new mauve-hued cloche hat on the closet shelf. That might be too much.

By the time she finished dressing, Nora realized that what she was doing was shedding the past with Jimmy and catching Lee Preston's admiring eye, even possibly greeting a promising future.

At eight o'clock that evening, Nora entered the Pine Inn's lobby. Waving at John Jordan, the hotel's friendly owner, standing behind the reservation desk, she headed in the direction of the hubbub that was coming from the hotel's dining room. With its polished oak floor, high ceiling and multi-paned windows along one wall looking out to Ocean Avenue and the beach on the far wall, the brightly lit room was packed with tourists, hotel guests and a bevy of her fellow Carmelites out on the town on Saturday evening.

Jenny, the pert hostess, who also played shortstop on Nora's softball team, greeted her with widened eyes. "Your dress is simply stunning. It's a big change from your uniform," she kidded. "Oh, I'm babbling, aren't I? Two guests are waiting for you to arrive. I'll take you straight to them." Leading the way, Jenny paused in the aisle between two candlelit tables and whispered, "All the men are staring and smiling at you, Nora. The women too. You look pretty as a picture."

"That's a very sweet thing to say, but I'm still the same old Nora that drops fly balls in left field."

Jenny giggled. "When Mr. Preston called for a reservation, he requested our best table. I hesitated until he told me that you were his special guest tonight. I like it when a man wants to make an impression on a lady."

Lee and Keith had been seated in front of the Inn's river rock fireplace. They stood up as the two women came up to the table. Nora saw that Keith had dressed for the occasion in a loose fitting tweed jacket, white shirt, red bow tie and tan, baggy trousers. By contrast, Lee's high-waisted, form-fitting, black jacket was more formal. A pale blue silk shirt, open at the throat, gave him a debonair look. His narrow, straight-legged slacks had the same sheen as his jacket.

Lee smiled as he pulled out the chair next to his and said, "You look beautiful, Nora. That outfit suits you perfectly. If you ever decide to give up your reporter's job, I'll find you one in Hollywood."

Nora took her seat and looked up at Jenny. The young woman was blushing. She appeared transfixed by Lee.

When he sat down, she stammered, "Enjoy your meal, Mr. Preston," and quickly retraced her steps to the hostess desk.

Nora was certain that her friend would want to hear all about the attractive stranger in town. She would share a few things with Jenny next time on the softball field.

"Is that a new hat?" Keith asked her. "I've never seen you wear it before. It has a distinctive Parisian flair."

Nora laughed. "I'd better stop poring over those French fashion magazines when I shop at the milliner's. Thank you both for the nice compliments."

Keith picked up a menu and began studying it. "Are you as starved as I am, Nora? I purposely didn't have lunch, knowing that my brother is paying for our meals. Isn't that right?"

Lee seemed surprised by Keith's question. "Of course. Both of you are my guests tonight."

Since Nora had first started working at the newspaper a year ago, she and Keith had become fast friends. She had been privy to the details of his infatuations with half a dozen eligible Carmel women. But between his full-time librarian's job and his part-time house painting work on weekends, he didn't have much free time or money to pursue any of them. He had confided to her that, since last December, he had been silently pining over one particular young lady by the name of Mayotta Brown.

Inexplicably, Keith jumped up and waved at a woman across the room. "What's she doing here?" he muttered. Excusing himself, he headed to a bank of tables next to the windows facing the street.

Lee put down his menu. He was visibly annoyed at his brother's brash behavior.

Nora turned around in her chair to watch Keith. He had stopped at the table occupied by Vera Winfield and James Carpenter.

"Isn't that your play's understudy over there with your director?" Lee asked.

Nora nodded and looked perplexed. "I've never heard Keith mention Vera's name — not once."

Lee shrugged. "Why would he suddenly become so attentive to her? For that matter, why would a woman like Vera be interested in my brother?"

Nora thought she could guess the reason. Out of the corner of her eye, she saw her fellow actor, Randall King, walk out of the kitchen, balancing a tray of hot food. He must be working his waiter's job tonight, she thought. At the same time, she noticed Keith taking Vera's elbow and ushering her back to their table.

"Hello, everyone," Vera cooed. She looked straight at Lee. "When I met Keith in front of the library earlier, he mentioned that he was having supper with his famous Hollywood screenwriter brother. I didn't expect to run into you here, Mr. Preston. It's a pleasure to see you again."

Getting up, Lee took Vera's extended hand. "Hello, Miss Winfield."

Nora noticed that the young woman didn't let go of it immediately.

Batting her heavily-made up eyelids, Vera said, "In case you're all wondering, I just couldn't say no to James tonight. After our rehearsal ended so abruptly, he insisted on taking me to dinner. The poor man's shocked about Guy Porter's murder. Of course, we all are."

Nora listened to the young woman's patter, all the while admiring her white silk dress accented with crystal sequins. *How could Vera buy that on her salary?* Nora had been coveting the classic sleeveless Jeanne Paquin design after seeing it in a fashion magazine at the dressmaker's shop last week. What interested her even more was how Vera had adjusted so quickly from grieving for Guy to having dinner with James, and now using Keith to cozy up to Lee. Did she even care for Guy, or was she play-acting this morning at Annie Stevens' boarding house? Her friend Claudia had it right. Vera was a true vamp.

The quiet hum of conversation was shattered by a loud voice coming from the other side of the dining room. "Just because your play might be canceled, don't think you can cheat me of what I'm owed!" Randall yelled. Hovering over James' table, the actor swayed back and forth, precariously balancing his tray over the director's head.

Nora heard James shout, "Don't threaten me! My play will go on as planned, if I have to take the lead role myself. Now go away and leave me alone."

Randall's voice got louder. "Tell that to the Forest Theater's board!"

Nora couldn't believe what she witnessed next.

James leaped out of his chair and pushed the actor in the

chest. Having to step back to maintain his balance, Randall lost his footing and dropped the tray of food on the floor. Both hands now free, he grabbed James by his suit's lapels and shook him.

Seeing all this, Lee said, "They're really serious. Excuse me, Nora. I'm going over to stop it before things get out of hand."

Nora said, "I'm coming too." She followed him across the room, just as James landed the first punch, knocking Randall to the ground. Rubbing his jaw and cursing under his breath, the actor got to his feet and, with his head down, bull-rushed into James' midsection. Both men fell to the floor, rolling over on one another, all the while, grunting and shouting obscenities.

By the time Lee and Nora reached them, the men had separated and were both on their knees, facing one another like two wild cats ready to pounce.

"Where are your manners?" Lee yelled. "If you can't behave like reasonable men, I'll have the management throw you both out of the hotel!"

"Keep out of this, Lee Preston," James barked. "I don't need any help from you."

Keith, who had followed closely behind Nora, grabbed Randall's arm and helped him up. "You don't want to lose your best-paying job, do you? Come outside with me."

Randall's face was showing the effects of the fist fight. Nora could see a black eye forming and the actor's lip was swollen.

Glaring at James, Randall said, "You owe me two months' salary for the time I put into your play. You agreed to pay for rehearsals. I have influence with Herbert Heron. I'll see to it that you won't have any of your plays put on at the Forest Theater."

Vera had come up. She put her arm around James and said, "Let's go."

Walking off together, the director shouted over his shoulder, "You're nothing but a hack actor, Randall. I'll be here long after you're old and forgotten."

For the moment, Vera had chosen to side with the director, Nora thought.

After the couple left the dining room by the side door, and Randall headed back to the kitchen, the dining room crowd that had been rapt and deadly silent resumed their humdrum murmurings. Nora, Lee and Keith walked back to their table and sat down.

"I'm even hungrier than I was before the scuffle," Keith grumbled. Picking up the menu, he said, "I hope there's enough food left in the kitchen. All I have at home is a tin of sardines, and now that the library's cat lives at the cabin with me, he has first dibs."

Nora smiled. "You should go to Leidig's. They're having a big sale on sardines." She knew why she liked Keith so much. His humor had lightened the moment.

Lee looked at Nora. "What James doesn't know is that his play is about to be canceled by the Forest Theater Society. Without a doubt, he'll try to change the board members' minds at their meeting tomorrow afternoon."

Nora said, "I didn't know the Society was meeting. Are you going to be there, Lee?" The reporter automatically reached for her purse, but realized that she had left her pad and pencil at home.

Lee nodded. "Yes. Mr. Heron invited me to attend. I have a stake in what happens, and I'll do all that I can to make sure that my play replaces Carpenter's. I've been told that, if the board members agree with Heron's opinion, mine will be staged at the Forest Theater in October."

Keith shook his head. "You mean to say that Randall won't be paid for his time? Then I don't blame him for demanding his money now. We're all barely scraping by. And does that mean that you'll get the hundred dollar prize money instead of Carpenter?"

"That will be up to the members of the board," Lee replied.

"I'm definitely going with you tomorrow," Nora said. "This will be a breaking story for my newspaper. Where and when?"

"It's been set for two o'clock at the Arts and Crafts Clubhouse on Casanova Street. Now let's forget about this for the time being. Shall we order our meal?"

"I thought you'd never get to that," Keith said, as he held up his menu and signaled to a nearby waiter.

After listening to the man's recitation of the nightly specials, Nora said, "I'll have the abalone with rice."

Lee put down his menu. "Coming from Charleston, I think I've heard of every conceivable creature that lives in the water, but not abalone. Is it a fish?"

Nora shook her head. "It's a mollusk and it's locally caught. You'll like it."

"I've eaten plenty of abalone," Keith said. It's nothing like those fresh oysters we shuck at home. I'm getting something closer to our Southern roots. I'll have the fried chicken and mashed potatoes with lots of gravy, waiter."

Nora said, "Let's try the strawberry shortcake for dessert."

The waiter nodded. "Good choice," he said, and walked to the kitchen.

An hour later, Keith pushed back from the table and said, "Would you two mind if I said goodnight? I've been on my feet, most of today, waiting on library patrons. All I can think of, besides my full stomach, is a walk before bed."

Lee chuckled. "Go ahead. I'll entertain Nora for as long as she allows me to."

Having walked Keith to the Pine Inn's front entrance, Nora and Lee returned to the hotel's lobby and sat together on a loveseat facing the Carmel stone fireplace. Watching the embers of pine logs glowing in the grate, Lee said, "This reminds me of home. I think I could get used to living in Carmel."

Nora decided this was a good time to ask Lee for some information. "What exactly went on at the San Francisco Bohemian Club between you and Guy Porter?"

"I knew you wouldn't forget," he teased. "All right, here goes. Last spring, I was invited, along with a few movie actors and directors, to travel up to San Francisco for some revelry at the Bohemian Club. It was their annual guests-invited weekend."

Nora interrupted, "Our play's director, James Carpenter, is a member of that group. Did you meet him there?"

"Matter of fact, I did. On our last night, we attended an outdoor party in the Bohemian Grove. Members' wives and escorts were included. I'm told that doesn't happen often. I ran into Guy Porter and James Carpenter after dinner and before the evening's entertainment started. We were all sitting at the bar, where home-brewed liquor was being served. I remind you that it's still Prohibition, but the police never once bothered us. We traded stories. I told them about my screenwriting work for the movies, and they talked about the theater. Before long, a woman joined us. James introduced her as his guest and said she was an actress. As the night wore on, Guy became unpleasant, probably because of having too much to drink."

"In what way?"

"He belittled her, saying she had only a tiny part in a play being produced at a theater on Sutter Street, and words to the effect that she would never be a star or have a lead part. That was evident when she left Hollywood. I thought he was overly critical of her. She simply laughed and said she would get better with his help."

"Let me take a wild guess. The young woman was Vera Winfield."

"Yes, and I was surprised to see that both of them were working here in Carmel."

Nora frowned. "Why did you pretend you didn't know her

when we were at the San Carlos Lodge this morning?"

"Southern manners dictate that a gentleman must protect a lady's reputation."

Looking up at the clock on the mantel, Nora said, "I'd like to talk longer, Lee, but I'd better be getting home. I'm due at the Carmel Mission at eight o'clock in the morning. My friends, Claudia and Rob Jacklin, invited me along to see the new religious piece that a local artist has sculpted."

Lee stood up. "I'd like to join you if don't mind. This is my first visit to Carmel, and I've heard so much about your mission from my parents. I'd really like to visit it."

Nora smiled. "They took Keith and me to a wonderful musical concert there the last time they visited him. You'll have to sit through a Catholic mass, which might be hard for you, since I've heard that all Southerners are Baptists."

He chuckled. "Not us Prestons. We've been Episcopalians for generations."

Embarrassed by her gaffe, Nora tried to cover her mistake by saying, "Before I forget all of my manners, I want to thank you for the delicious dinner. I've really enjoyed this pleasant evening."

"I feel the same, and I can vouch for Keith that he had a good time too."

They left the hotel. The trip to Pine Log, Nora's cottage, took five minutes. No one said anything until Lee had cut the motor.

Nora spoke first. "I hesitate to ask, but are you willing to teach me to drive?"

"Of course, I am. I know we've just met, but I'm very drawn to you."

His words troubled Nora. She said, "Truthfully, I'm not looking for a new beau. I've just broken up with a young man and my feelings are still tender."

Before she could object, she felt Lee's arm go around her shoulders. He pulled her close to him and then suddenly released her.

Studying her face, he said, "You'd better go inside, or I can't be responsible for what happens next."

Waving at him as he turned the Cadillac around and headed back to the hotel, Nora wondered what would have happened if he had stayed with her a minute longer.

CHAPTER TEN

Sunday

Getting into the passenger seat of Lee's automobile, Nora said, "I'll be happy to show you the way to the Carmel Mission this morning, but at the same time, I'm planning to watch your every move."

Her comment took him aback. "Why is that? Have I done something that leads you to distrust me?"

"No, it isn't that. It's because I'm looking forward to having you teach me how to drive."

Lee laughed out loud. "I don't know what you can pick up by observation, Nora. The real learning comes when you get behind the wheel yourself."

"What do you think the hardest part is going to be?"

"That's easy. Learning how to shift the gears."

Nora pursed her lips. "Well, I'm very eager to try."

Turning on the starter, Lee moved the gear shift and accelerated.

Following her directions, he pulled into the last parking space near a sign that read: Mission San Carlos de Borromeo Del Rio Carmelo. Nora took a silk scarf out of her purse and put it over her head. They entered the aging adobe structure and found seats on the last bench at the back, just as Father Ramon Mestres and two altar boys came into the sanctuary through a side door. The priest blessed the congregation and began speaking in Latin. Although she had studied the language at Mills College, Nora hadn't retained enough to understand him, although several hymns sung by a children's choir sounded familiar to her. One of the altar boys, who knelt behind the priest, began swinging a small gold canister on a long chain. From it came the aroma of burning incense. Sneaking a peek at Lee, Nora whispered, "What's your impression of the ritual we're watching?"

"I see comparisons to my Anglican faith. I think it's beautifully presented."

When a tinkling bell sounded, worshippers began filing up the aisle. Both Nora and Lee bowed their heads and stayed seated while the parishioners walked up to the railing in front of the altar to take Holy Communion.

After the mass was over, "Nora stood up and said, "Let's go outside and find the Jacklin family. They're expecting us."

Everyone in the sunny courtyard was milling about and jabbering loudly. Taking Lee's arm, Nora guided him to her friends, who were waiting in the center of the plaza. She said, "Hello, Claudia and Rob. This is Lee Preston, Keith's brother."

"It's nice to meet you," Rob said, stepping up and shaking Lee's hand. "You drive a beautiful car. I saw you with Nora yesterday at the softball field. How long will you be staying in Carmel, Mr. Preston?"

"I'm not sure. I guess for as long as Miss Finnegan can put up with me."

They all laughed.

Nora said, "Where's Freddie? On the telephone you said he was over his fever."

"He is," Claudia replied. "He's playing over there by the tiled fountain."

Nora turned to see the undersized, eleven-year-old standing on tiptoes and dipping his hands in the water. She and Lee walked over to him. "Freddie, I'm delighted to see that you're feeling better today," she said. "I want you to meet Mr. Preston."

Drying his hands on the front of his pants, Freddie extended his right hand to Lee.

"You've got a strong grip, Freddie," Lee said. "You know a man's measured by his handshake."

The boy looked puzzled. "Are you a relative of Mr. Preston, the librarian?"

"You bet I am. We're brothers, and I'm guessing you probably read lots of adventure stories that he recommends."

Freddie nodded. "He picks out good ones." Turning to Nora, he said, "Guess what? I'm going to be Rob's new son and take his last name. He's adopting me."

"Oh, that's wonderful news." Nora said, as she ruffled his wispy blond hair.

The three then drifted back to where Claudia and Rob were standing.

"I heard Freddie talking about the adoption," Rob said, as they walked up.

"We're excited too." Putting his arm around his wife's waist, he added, "Claudia and I are doing the paperwork together. It should all be legal in a month or so."

Full of energy, Freddie was jumping up and down. He said, "Dad, can Nora and her friend come with us to see Father Serra's statue?"

Patting Freddie's head to calm him, Rob said, "I think Nora already made plans to do just that."

"Your dad's right," Nora said. "Matter of fact, I'm writing a feature story for my newspaper about today's dedication. It's an important occasion, which is why I was so pleased when your parents asked me to accompany them."

"I'm going to take my own pictures," Freddie crowed. He pointed to the box camera that was dangling from a strap around his neck. "Rob, I mean, Dad, bought this for me at Levy's general store yesterday. He's going to show me how to use it and then we're going to develop my pictures in his dark room behind our house."

"If they turn out," Nora said, "I'll ask Mr. Owens to put one of them in the *Pine Cone* along with my article." Nora was pleased to see how happy Freddie was, after what had been a very difficult time for him a year ago after his real father died.

Joining in the enthusiasm of the moment, Lee said, "There might be an idea for a screenplay that I can make up after seeing the dedication this morning. Where is Father Serra's statue, Freddie? Is it far from this mission?"

The boy looked up at his mother, unsure of the answer.

"It's not too far — that is, if you travel by automobile," Claudia said.

Nora smiled at Freddie. "We'll be driving there too. Would you like to ride with us?"

"That's a good idea," Lee said. "The boy can show me how to get there."

"Say yes, Mama!"

"That's fine. I feel it's so special that we can all drive from the mission to the statue today. This might interest you for your story, Nora. Legend has it that Father Serra actually walked the same route we'll be taking to his new statue. I'm guessing it's probably close to an hour's hike."

"I too have some news for your article," Rob said. "The sculptor who created Serra's image in wood will be there. His name's Jo Mora."

Everyone stopped talking, as Father Mestres, clad in a black cassock, stepped out of the church. "Let's meet up with the rest of the crowd in the village," he shouted.

Sitting in the Cadillac's back seat, Freddie, with Nora's help, directed Lee to the Carmel Woods area and Serra's statue at the northern edge of town. Dozens of people had already arrived. Lee found a parking place in a grassy meadow at the end of a row of cars. "Where are we exactly?" he asked Nora. "Is this area still part of the village?"

"No, Carmel is only a mile in size. This is a new subdivision that Samuel F. B. Morse, a Pebble Beach developer, is building. But I'm curious about something, Lee," Nora said, as she helped Freddie out of the car. "Do you happen to know Edward Kuster, the prominent Los Angeles attorney? He's active with the Serra Pageant Committee and he should be at this morning's dedication. He has been talking about building a new indoor theater in Carmel. I think you should meet him."

Lee didn't respond immediately. Then he said, "I already know him. I'll explain how we met, but it has to wait for a later time."

"Why not tell me now?"

Before he could answer, the Jacklins, walking hand in hand, came up. "Did you have fun riding in Mr. Preston's car, dear?" Claudia asked.

The boy ran toward her, his camera bumping up and down on his chest. "I'm going to buy a Cadillac just like Mr. Preston's when I get older," he yelled.

"Please lower your voice," his mother said, then added, "Nora, we Catholics don't eat breakfast before taking communion, so I've brought along a thermos of hot tea and some extra cups. I hope you and Lee will join us."

"Did you remember the cinnamon buns you made, Mama?" Freddie interrupted.

Claudia smiled. "Now, what do you think?" she teased.

They began walking toward the crowd that was gathering at the place where the street formed a junction with several other dirt roads.

Staring up at the shrine, with its life-size statue perched on a stone platform under a tile-roofed canopy, Nora wondered how long it had taken Jo Mora to carve Serra's image out of solid oak.

Father Mestres held up his hand, apparently ready to introduce the dignitaries. Nora took out her pad and pencil and began writing down the names and titles of those present, taking notice of one particular couple, Edward and Ruth Kuster. To her surprise, Mr. Kuster motioned to Lee.

Excusing himself, Lee walked over to the older man, shook hands with him, and exchanged a few words.

When he returned, he looked excited, but said nothing to Nora.

Nudging him, she said, "I'm being nosy, but what did you two talk about?"

Lee's face looked non-committal. "You can find out when we go to the Forest Theater Society's meeting this afternoon."

"That's a long time to wait, Mr. Preston."

"All right then. I'll give you a little tidbit to keep you interested."

"Is it something I can add to my news story?"

"That depends on you."

Turning to a new page in her notepad, Nora stared up at him. "Are we playing some game? Why so secretive?"

Leaning closer, he said, "Secret number one. I just remembered where I first heard Jo Mora's name. It was at the San Francisco Bohemian Club. Mora created a memorial plaque for the famous author, Bret Harte. I told Mr. Kuster that it's on the wall near the Club's front entrance. Secret number two. Guy Porter pointed it out to me the night I was there."

"I can't believe that you and Kuster talked about that."

Just then, Nora felt a hand on her shoulder. Turning around, she recognized the familiar face. "Hello, Marshal," she said. "I didn't know you were coming today."

Gus Englund tipped his hat. "I couldn't help but overhear Mr. Preston mention Guy Porter's name. If you're still working on the story, I have the latest piece of news."

"I haven't turned it in yet."

"Good," Englund said. "Sheriff Connery telephoned me before I left home to ride up here. He said he's arrested Victor Wolfe for Porter's murder. He and Deputy Jensen have taken him to the Monterey jail. The sheriff wants to interview you, Mr. Preston. He says for you to be at my office tomorrow morning at eight o'clock sharp. Now I think we'd better stop gabbing and listen to what the padre has to say."

CHAPTER ELEVEN

The Forest Theater Society's meeting was scheduled for two o'clock. Nora left Pine Log fifteen minutes early and walked to the Arts and Crafts Clubhouse on Casanova Street. She always thought the one-story, barn-shingled building resembled an oversized, one-room cottage with an expansive wood floor and a large Carmel stone fireplace. As usual, chairs were stacked along the back of the room. Today someone had placed a dozen of them in two rows at the front.

Nora recalled the times when she and her parents had come here to attend plays, view painting exhibits, and enjoy musical recitals since the hall's construction in 1907. However, one memory stood out. Last Valentine's Day, she and Jimmy Connery had attended a special formal ball in this room. Both of them had dressed up for the occasion and Jimmy had splurged on a corsage. They had danced the fox trot and the Charleston past midnight. She felt a little sad that Jimmy had decided not to be friendly to her.

Putting aside her musings, she chose a seat in the front row facing several chairs and a makeshift table, consisting of a door placed on top of a pair of sawhorses. Nora recognized the two men, deep in conversation, who were standing behind the table.

Both of them directed plays and were dedicated theater people. The taller man was slender, with a prominent nose, high forehead, dark eyes, and curly black hair. The other was stocky and rugged looking, with a shock of fair hair and weathered skin. Herbert Heron was the handsomer of the two, Nora thought, although Perry Newberry had a rough and ready charm.

Each man had considerable influence in village affairs. Heron was a classical actor who had founded the Forest Theater Society, and also owned a rare book business. Newberry was a journalist who built cottages all over Carmel. Recently, he had been elected to the post of the city's Board of Trustees.

"Hello, Nora," Lee said, as he came up and took the aisle seat next to her. "You look relaxed after our outing to the Serra shrine. And I might add, pretty as ever."

"I appreciate the compliment; however, I don't feel the least bit rested. I've been poring over my notes on Guy Porter's murder. I just can't believe that Victor Wolfe could do such a wretched thing."

"After dropping you off, I went back to my hotel room and prepared a brief presentation about my play."

She noticed that he avoided discussing the murder. "Yes, it seems we've both been busy," she said.

"Mr. Heron has asked me to speak after the play committee's decision is made public. I'll be glad when this is all over."

"I will too, because I need to finish my article before tomorrow morning."

"Let's take a break tonight and see the movie that's showing at Manzanita Hall."

Nora smiled. "How did you hear about that?"

"I saw a man driving a pony cart down Ocean Avenue on the way over here. He had a hand-painted sign propped up on the back of the cart that said: Movie Tonight."

"That was Delos Curtis, and I'll bet his dog Bruno was

running alongside him, wasn't he? Those two are a fixture in the village."

Lee grinned. "I've never seen such simple advertising be so effective. Tell me you'll go to the movies with me later on."

Nora didn't answer. She saw that Heron and Newberry, now sitting at the table, appeared ready to start.

In a loud voice, Heron called out, "For those of you who are just arriving, there are several seats in the front. I'm calling this meeting to order."

Nora saw James Carpenter, Panama hat in hand, come forward and seat himself at the other end of the front row. The director looked over at them and scowled.

"I think he knows that his play is about to be replaced," Lee said.

"How can you tell that?"

"You forget that I've seen a lot of movie actors. They can show you what they're thinking by simply raising an eyebrow, curling a lip, or twitching their noses."

Nora was amused by his words. Somehow, she felt comfortable being with Lee.

Leaning over, she whispered, "I do want to go to the movies tonight."

Herbert Heron got to his feet. "There has been a decision to change the winning play for this year's annual competition," he said. "Perry, will you give the committee's report?"

"Be happy to," Newberry said, as he stood up. "The Forest Theater Society's annual competition always produces excellent plays, including this year's first prize winner, "A Shadow Falls on Justice." Initially, the play committee thought it would be popular with audiences and financially successful. Unfortunately, that has changed."

James Carpenter got to his feet. "Wait until you hear me out."

Heron pounded on the table with his fist. "Hold your thoughts until Perry's finished," he said, motioning Carpenter to sit down.

Newberry looked out at the audience and continued, "When Mr. Carpenter decided to go against local tradition and hire an outsider for the starring role, many of our fellow Carmelites became angry and threatened to boycott his production. But the committee decided not to take action at that time. However, yesterday, the play's lead actor was murdered. The committee sympathizes with the director and his actors, who have all worked hard to this point. But we believe the Forest Theater Society cannot risk the negative publicity and rumors that surround this play. A resulting lack of attendance would be devastating to the theater's financial status."

Heron interrupted, "Let me add something, Perry. Everyone in town knows that you and I have had our disagreements in the past, but I wholly support you and the play committee on this one a hundred percent."

"Thank you. Let me conclude by saying that a financial loss can't be absorbed. The Society made a modest profit on two of the three plays produced last season, but we can't take a chance this time. We have to protect the Forest Theater from any possible fiscal insolvency."

As Newberry sat down, Heron looked straight at Carpenter. "James, it's my duty to inform you that your play is cancelled. We also voted to substitute the one awarded second place. That playwright is here at my invitation."

Lee got up and walked over to the director. "No hard feelings, sir," he said. "I'm very sorry that your play is being shut down."

Nora saw the anger on Carpenter's face. He rose to his feet, brushed off Lee's proffered hand and said, "I don't agree with the financial problems you two men foresee, and I don't accept your ill-formed, hasty decision. Yes, Guy Porter is dead, but his understudy is replacing him. Victor Wolfe is a fine local actor. He's been at every rehearsal. He knows Porter's lines. Opening night is going forward as planned next weekend. I predict that we will have a full house."

"You don't understand," Heron said. "Our decision is final. You are to vacate the theater. If you choose not to, then our city marshal will make sure that you do."

"I'll be damned if I will!" Carpenter shouted.

"I've got my orders, Mr. Heron," a voice said from the back of the clubhouse.

Nora turned around and saw Marshal Gus Englund standing by the door. Apparently, Heron had anticipated there would be some reaction from the director.

Carpenter threw up his hands. "This is insane," he muttered for everyone to hear.

Perry Newberry spoke up. "It's time we heard from Mr. Preston. Give us a synopsis of what you've written, young man. If I recall, it's a children's play. That's going to make my wife Bertha very happy, since she's written one herself."

"Thank you," Lee said, and remained standing. He took a folded crème-colored paper from his pocket.

Nora recognized the Pine Inn's stationery.

Unfolding the notepaper, Lee began, "My play's title is: *The Captain and the Caterpillar*. Set fifty years ago in the 1870s, it's about a boy growing up in the San Joaquin Valley. His family comes to Fresno to homestead land after the destruction of their plantation in Mississippi during the Civil War. The young boy comes of age while experiencing all the hardships of farming for a living. He loves driving all the farm machinery and is nicknamed Caterpillar. It's a drama, sometimes sad, yet often laced with the humorous perspective of an innocent boy facing life's adventures."

Carpenter jumped up and shook his fist at Heron and

Newberry. "I can't believe you men would think of dishonoring the excellent reputation of the Western Drama Society. Have you forgotten we were formed by such literary giants as Jack London and George Sterling? Lee Preston's children's play doesn't rise to their high standards. My play does. There is no reason whatsoever to cancel it."

"I disagree," Lee said, turning to Carpenter. "They have one very important reason. Your understudy, Victor Wolfe — the actor you say can assume your leading man's role — was arrested this morning by the Monterey County Sheriff on suspicion of Guy Porter's murder. The marshal at the back of the room can verify that."

A red-faced Carpenter shouted, "I wrote the damn play. I can play the part myself. I'm calling my lawyer." Getting up, the director stormed out of the Clubhouse.

Lee put the notepaper in his pocket and smiled at Nora.

She could see unbridled satisfaction on his face.

CHAPTER TWELVE

Monday

William Owens hung up the telephone receiver as Nora walked through the *Carmel Pine Cone's* front door. "Just the person I've been waiting for," he said, as he came over to the counter. "Sheriff Connery's been asking for you."

"Was that him on the telephone?"

"No, that was my mother-in-law. She said that Mary Lee and Sally have left Chicago and are on their way home. They'll be back on Wednesday."

"That's wonderful news," Nora said. She too missed his wife. Stacks of invoices, receipts and sundry notices that Mrs. Owens would have filed away lay in a neglected basket on the counter. "What did Jimmy want with me?" she asked.

"All he said was that you should expect him to stop by the office sometime after lunch. And he stressed the word *after*. Since you two broke up, I guess he's through wanting to talk to you at the Blue Bird."

Nora recalled the numerous lunches she and Jimmy had shared at the local tea room. Frowning, she said, "I don't know why that man thinks I'm at his beck and call."

Owens laughed. "He's merely asserting his authority, since

being promoted."

"Perhaps, but I hope he's civil to me when he does show up."

"Aside from Jimmy, what I'm more interested in is whether you have the Porter story ready for me. Tommy Anderson's cooling his heels in the back room. He's waiting to post our special edition on the town bulletin board and deliver papers to subscribers."

Opening her purse, Nora took out several sheets of notepaper and handed them to him. "I'm sorry all of this is hand-written, but I worked on it at home last night."

Owens put on his glasses, scanned her writing, and said, "It's legible." Then, looking at her more closely, he added, "You have dark circles under your eyes. If Mrs. Owens were here, she would be worried about you."

"Keith's brother took me to see the Lillian Gish movie at Manzanita Hall last night. After I got home, I stayed up late to finish that story you're holding."

Owens wrinkled his nose. "Mary Lee and I saw that film about unrequited love. She liked it, but I call it pure hogwash. I hope you don't have any appointments this morning, Honora. I want you to answer the telephone while I finish the printing job."

"That's fine, but it will set me back if I have to stay past twelve o'clock. I'm visiting Burt Erickson on my lunch hour. I want to find out how he is and if he suspects who assaulted him at the theater Friday night. I also plan to stop at the lumberyard."

"If the printing press doesn't act up, I'll set the type and do a run before noon. If not, you need to stay." Owens turned around and headed for the back room.

Seated at her desk, Nora busied herself answering the telephone. In between calls, she filed a week's worth of classified advertisements. She happened to notice one that Mr. Owens had written up earlier before she had arrived for work:

AUDITIONS FOR "THE CAPTAIN & THE CATERILLAR"

AN ORIGINAL LELAND PRESTON CHILDREN'S PLAY

OCTOBER PERFORMANCES AT THE FOREST THEATER

PROSPECTIVE ACTORS INTERVIEWED THIS WED. 6-8 P.M.

Lee Preston must have brought his classified ad in before going to City Hall for his interview with the sheriff, she thought. Already her imagination was fueling the dread she would experience when she had to meet with Jimmy one-on-one later today.

Nora left the newspaper office at twelve-thirty. She was glad to see that the fog had lifted. Bright sunshine elevated her mood. She knew that Burt Erickson lived in a cabin behind the corner house at Mission and Tenth Avenue. Walking up the driveway toward the rundown structure, she saw the prop man on the front porch. Eyes closed, he was rocking back and forth in a weather-beaten rocking chair. Blackie, his old Labrador, lay asleep at his feet. The dog woke up and barked once when Nora called out, "How are you feeling today, Burt?"

Opening his eyes, he said, "Hello, miss. I'm better, but this darned bandage that Doc Barnes put on me at the theater itches like crazy."

"That's a good sign. It means your wound is healing. Has anyone told you the news that our play has been cancelled?"

"Tommy Anderson stopped by and told me last night. He brought me a bowl of chili his ma made. I plan to heat it up and have it for lunch in a little while."

"That sounds good. I, too, wanted to see how you were feeling and also ask you a couple of questions, if that's all right. I'm writing a story that describes your assault. Maybe someone who reads it will have some ideas as to the person who did it."

"Well, I certainly don't know. Marshal Englund came by yesterday and I told him I didn't see who hit me and I didn't notice any strangers around the theater."

Nora reached into her purse and took out paper and pencil. "Why don't you start by telling me everything you did last Friday before the cast arrived?"

Leaning back, Burt relaxed. "First, I took down the scenery from the previous play rehearsal and swept the stage clean. Then I put up the set for your play. I hope you don't write anything about the piece of scenery falling on the sofa where Mr. Porter was sitting. Mr. Carpenter already gave me what-for about that."

Nora smiled. "That was an accident, Burt — nothing more. Go on, please."

"O. K. I went back to the shed, and being it was a full dress rehearsal, Mr. Carpenter had ordered real milk for your tea service. I brought a pint from home and put it on ice to keep it fresh. The tea tray was on the bench where I usually leave it. I decided I would get to it after I polished the justice scale Mr. Carpenter was nagging me about. I was working on that when somebody socked me in the head."

"So you never put the milk in the pitcher that night, much less fixed my tray?"

"I sure didn't. I guess the milk from home is still in the ice bucket under my bench. It's probably spoiled by now. You know, I count on Mr. Carpenter's paycheck each week. I'm worried what's going to happen, now that the play's shut down."

"The theater's directors have decided to substitute a new play. Unfortunately, they won't start rehearsals right away."

"You think they'll need someone like me to build scenery and set things up?"

"With your experience, you'll surely get the job. If you need a small loan to tide you over, I have money saved."

Burt looked embarrassed. "Heck, no, miss. I've got a little of my own stashed away, but you're sure nice to offer it. I won't forget that."

Getting ready to go, Nora said, "You should see Doctor Barnes today and have him put a new dressing on your head."

For the first time, he smiled. "I will, miss. I have an appointment this afternoon."

Looking at her watch, Nora saw that it was after one o'clock. If Sheriff Connery had arrived at the newspaper office, he would simply have to wait. It was more important that she talk to Carmel's brick mason, Benjamin Turner.

Arriving at the large fenced area at the eastern end of town, Nora read the sign over the gated entry: M. J. Murphy Lumber and Building Supplies. On all sides of her were rows of flat boards and wood beams neatly stored at eye level the length of the lot. Other piles of bricks, stone, and sand were interspersed among the numerous stacks of lumber. Coming up to the yard superintendent, she inquired as to the brick mason's whereabouts.

"He's working over at the San Carlos Lodge today, ma'am," the man said.

As she came up Annie Stevens' walk and entered her front garden, Nora recognized the short, husky man in bib coveralls. Standing to one side of a low, half-built wall, Ben Turner was drinking water from a thermos bottle. The man had repaired her cottage's chimney last year. She said, "Hi, Mr. Turner. Remember me? It's Nora Finnegan. I know you're working, but do you mind if I ask you a few questions?"

Putting down his drink, and drying his hands on his pants, he said, "Hello, Miss Finnegan. I fixed your folks' fireplace a while back. Is it drawing like it should?"

"It's working just fine, thanks to you."

He smiled. "Seems like we're getting into a warm spell, doesn't it? When I work outdoors on a project like this, I appreciate the days we have fog."

"I don't want to take up too much of your time. I'm here because one of the stage actors at the Forest Theater was murdered over the weekend."

"I heard about that. The missus and I think it's a shame, him being so young."

"Doc Staniford at the drug store found muriatic acid in some liquid that Mr. Porter drank. I thought of you when Doc told me that muriatic acid is used to clean bricks. Has your supply been tampered with?"

"I keep it in the shed behind my house. Far as I can tell, nobody's disturbed it. Say, if you're interested in seeing muriatic acid at work, I have something to show you."

Nora was puzzled. "Why do you need it for this job, Mr. Turner? It looks like you're building a stucco wall for Mrs. Stevens, not a brick one."

He laughed. "Come with me and I'll explain."

Leading the way to Annie's back yard, Turner stopped in front of a row of large, wide-mouth clay pots. Each was tightly covered.

Prying opening the lid of the nearest one, he said, "Take a peek inside. This one contains muriatic acid."

Stepping closer, Nora looked down. A pungent odor rose from the clear liquid. "Except for the smell, it looks harmless to me."

Turner covered it by firming down the lid. He pried open the next one. "What do you see?"

Nora peered into the open container. "I see abalone shells covered with kelp. They sure smell fishy! Where did you get all these shells?"

"Annie's been collecting them for months. She goes down the coast to Whalers Cove where the Japanese abalone divers discard them after removing the meat."

"Are the rest of these closed pots filled with shells?"

"That's right. They've been soaking in water for three days. This afternoon, I'll put on rubber gloves, and using a pair of tongs, take them out of the water and drop them for about a minute in the pot with the acid. It eats away the kelp. All I have to do then is wash off the acid, brush the residue off with water from a hose, and I've got a pretty abalone shell ready to embed and decorate the base of Annie's new stucco wall."

"That acid works quickly. I saw what happened on the Forest Theater's stage. The acid and milk mixture that spilled on the floor immediately caused a hole in the rug."

"That's not surprising, since it's so corrosive. I feel sorry for that fellow who swallowed it."

"I'm glad I spoke with you, Mr. Turner. What you've described will make my follow-up story on the murder more interesting to my readers."

As she hurried back to the newspaper office, Nora realized that the "lethal weapon" that had been used to kill Guy Porter was similar to a gun — very available and very dangerous in the wrong hands.

CHAPTER THIRTEEN

Nora spotted Sheriff Jimmy Connery through the *Pine Cone's* front window. He was standing at the counter and reading her front page story about Guy Porter's murder. Dark-haired, broad-shouldered, and just under six feet tall, his handsome features still held an unmistakable attraction. A shiny, star-shaped sheriff's badge adorned the front of his lawman's uniform. His presence made her very uncomfortable.

He looked up and put down the newspaper as she closed the door. "Mr. Owens told me you were out on an assignment," he said. "Good thing you showed up. I was getting ready to leave."

"Sorry to keep you waiting, Sheriff." Nora felt his blue eyes following her as she walked across the room to store her purse in her desk's bottom drawer.

Pointing at the *Pine Cone* on the counter, he said. "You seem almost too familiar with the details surrounding Mr. Porter's death."

Nora couldn't tell if he was complimenting her or accusing her of revealing too much information. "I try to be as accurate as possible in my reporting."

"I remember. Of course. Your career is your highest priority. Let's not waste any more of my time. Mr. Owens said that we can meet in his private office. He'll be working at another desk in the back room."

As she had expected, this would be a strained meeting for both of them. Leading the way to the publisher's office, Nora felt a chill course through her body. Brushing past her, Jimmy sat down in Owens' swivel chair, while Nora had to pull a straight back chair into the room from the hall.

Dropping his Stetson on top of the desk, he said, "You had the role of the maid in the play rehearsal, Miss Finnegan, and as such, you had direct contact with the cream pitcher full of the poisonous substance that led to Mr. Porter's murder. In my book, that makes you a potential suspect."

Unable to control herself, Nora's voice rose. "You're holding a grudge against me, Jimmy, and it doesn't suit you."

William Owens came out into the hall when he heard her voice. "Are you all right, Honora?" he yelled through the closed door.

"I'm fine," Nora said, while struggling to regain her composure.

Neither said anything for several minutes. Finally, Jimmy muttered, "I've been unprofessional, Nora. I know you couldn't kill anyone. It's just that I've felt so angry with you since we parted. As I drove here from Monterey this morning, all I could think of was how to punish you for rejecting me as a husband."

Nora leaned back, relieved that the pressure of their first encounter had eased. She said, "I'm sorry too, Jimmy. Truthfully, after getting to know you so well, the last thing I wanted was to hurt you. You're ready for marriage and I'm not. Your young daughter Molly deserves a fulltime mother. I can't take on such an important role right now because my reporter's job here at the *Pine Cone* is what I want most."

He looked away. "It's hard for me to accept that. Why don't we get to our interview? I met with Lee Preston several hours ago

and listened to his story which points to Victor Wolfe, Guy Porter's understudy, as the likely murder suspect. Mr. Preston said
that you'll verify that the man he saw at the theater was Wolfe."

"From the description Mr. Preston provided me, it could
only be Victor."

"I agree with you. Also, Wolfe admits that he did what
Preston described him doing in the interval between the two play
rehearsals. But he claims he was just getting a drink of water."

"Are you still keeping him in custody?"

"Yes, because he doesn't have a verifiable alibi for his
whereabouts in the early hours of Saturday morning. That's when
Doctor Barnes estimates that Porter was attacked and killed. By
the way, what can you tell me about this fellow, Lee Preston?"

"His brother is a friend of mine, Jimmy. Keith introduced
us last Friday night. I've since learned that Lee is a successful
Hollywood screenwriter. He's come to Carmel to see his first
play produced at the Forest Theater."

"I know all of that. What I'm referring to is whether Preston
is trying to influence you. He told me that he took you to dinner.
That he drove you all over town this past weekend. That you two
even went to a movie last night. He said that he finds you very
friendly and cooperative. So what do you think of him?"

Nora's face flushed. "That's a personal matter! I thought we
were discussing a murder. Let's talk about solving that. I have
something to show you that is far more important than discussing
Lee Preston. It means that we have to go to the Forest Theater
now."

"This had better not be a wild goose chase. I don't have any
time to waste."

"It's less than a ten minute walk. That is, if you can spare
that much time."

Jimmy grinned. "All right, let's call a truce." Standing up
and putting on his Stetson, he said, "I wouldn't mind walking

through the village with you, Nora, and it would be nice to breathe in some fresh ocean air."

"Agreed. I'll go back and let Mr. Owens know where we're going."

"I've never seen the Forest Theater so deserted," Nora said. "Of course, I've never come here on a weekday afternoon either."

Passing the shuttered ticket booth, she and Jimmy followed a worn path behind the stage to an outbuilding nestled under the trees.

"This is where our scenery and props are kept," Nora said. Opening the door and stepping inside, she added, "It should be right over here where our prop man, Burt Erickson, told me he left it."

"Left what? You're full of surprises. What exactly are we looking for?"

Kneeling down and reaching into a bucket of water under the prop man's workbench, Nora brought out a pint-sized bottle. Standing up, she smiled and handed it to Jimmy. "This is the milk bottle that Burt transported from home to the theater. It was to be used during our dress rehearsal Friday night. Open it, and tell me if it's fresh."

Pulling off the lid's cover, Jimmy sniffed the bottle's contents. "It's sour," he said, and made a face. "I'm confused. You'd better explain what you're getting at."

"Not yet. We need to go to another spot before I do. Follow me."

Nora led him back to the outdoor stage, where she had spent many an evening. She motioned him to follow her on stage and paused where her tea tray once sat.

Coming up to stand next to her, Jimmy said, "Why in God's name are we here?"

Nora stepped over to the edge of the stage. "While waiting

for my cue last Friday night, I noticed something odd. However, at the time, I didn't think much of it."

Joining her, Jimmy stared down at the ground below the stage. "I don't see anything except a pile of pine cones."

"Look just past them to the right. See that place where the light is reflecting?" Nora pointed to a glass object, half-hidden by a low ceonothus bush. "Even from this height, I recognize the label," she said.

He shrugged. "What's so important about an empty milk bottle?"

"That bottle was purchased from Leidig Brothers grocery store. The bottle in the tub had no label. It was delivered by truck to the milk shrine near Burt Erickson's home. I think you should go down there, Jimmy, and pick this one up with your handkerchief. If I'm right, the fingerprints on this bottle will belong to Victor Wolfe."

"Much as I hate to admit it, Nora, you never cease to amaze me."

CHAPTER FOURTEEN

Tuesday

"*Carmel Pine Cone*. Miss Finnegan speaking. How may I help you this morning?"

"Hello, Nora. It's Julia. How are you? I've missed you these past few weeks."

"Julia! I've missed you too." The voice of San Francisco architect Julia Morgan lifted Nora's spirits. "I wanted to contact you, but when we last spoke on the telephone, you were in the midst of handling a difficult construction problem at San Simeon."

"I'm afraid it continues to demand my attention."

"What about the supervisor you hired from Monterey? Has he met your needs?"

"Henry Washburn is very competent, but given a crew of forty-four men and the complex nature of my building plans for Mr. Hearst's residence, his job is challenging. I always visit San Simeon on weekends so that I can stay on top of everything."

"How exciting, to see your vision become a reality. But where are you now?"

"I'm in Pacific Grove, where I'm staying the night. I'm calling in hopes that you're free this evening, Nora. I know it's short notice, but I've become involved in a crisis of sorts at the Y.W.C.A. encampment at Asilomar."

"I hope nothing serious has happened to you."

"Not to me. All I'll say on the telephone is that a young lady who is staying here is having personal problems. When I was told about them, I immediately thought of you. You could be very helpful if you can meet me tonight. If so, I'll have my driver pick you up at Pine Log at six o'clock, and explain things over supper at the Crocker dining hall."

"I'll be ready, Julia. I'll see you this evening."

"That's wonderful. And by the way, you needn't dress up."

Nora put down the receiver and felt a surge of happiness wash over her. The thought of being in her mentor's company for a few hours was something to look forward to. She wondered if the young woman Julia had spoken about was trying to convince her parents to let her follow a career path, as she had done. Returning to her desk, she went to work on Burt Erickson's assault story and performed some necessary clerical tasks in Mrs. Owens' absence.

It was close to two o'clock, when Nora arrived at City Hall at the northwest corner of Ocean Avenue and Dolores Street. Entering by the side door, she took the stairs to the second floor meeting room. Mr. Owens had given her the task of reporting on Carmel's Planning Commission meetings. The Board of Trustees had appointed the group only last February. Their charge was to guide and monitor all building projects that were changing the village's appearance. Nora found the assignment unique, since the new Commissioners also served as the Civic Committee for the Arts and Crafts Club. She applauded their efforts to protect and promote the residents' interests.

Finding a place in the first row reserved for "Members of the Press," Nora took out some paper and a pencil. She noted that all five of the Commissioners were present. Turning around in her seat, she surveyed the audience.

Standing off to one side, Carmel's policeman, Marshal Gus

Englund, was listening to an irate citizen argue over a recent traffic ticket. When he noticed Nora, Englund extricated himself from the conversation and strolled down the side aisle to where she was seated. "Good afternoon, Miss Finnegan," he said. "Anything interesting on today's planning agenda?"

Scanning the list of typed items that she had received from the city clerk, Nora said, "Except for the usual requests for tree removals, installing fences, and replacing tent cabins with permanent roofing and windows, there is one other topic that always makes for a lively discussion. It's a subject that comes up frequently."

"Let me guess. Fire Chief Nichols arrived a few minutes ago. I assume he's here to ask once again that our residential cottages all be numbered."

Nora chuckled. "You and I both know that his request will never be granted, even though it's a matter of safety. Chief Nichols realizes that Carmelites enjoy giving their homes all sorts of personal names. It's laudable that he never gives up." Referring back to the agenda, Nora put up her hand. "But wait a minute. Someone has hand-written a few words down at the bottom."

"What do they say?"

"I'm not sure what 'Chairman's Discretionary Item' refers to, Marshal. Do you know?"

Englund shrugged. "Maybe it's about City Hall sharing larger accommodations with the post office in their new building on Dolores Street. I'm not happy with having to move either. I like being centrally located here on Ocean Avenue, although things are getting a bit crowded."

"I suppose we'll have to wait and see. By the way, I've been meaning to ask you something. Do you have any new leads on who might have injured Burt Erickson? I'm writing a follow-up story on his assault for this week's edition of the paper."

"No, unfortunately. I'm hoping the fingerprints on that

milk bottle you found for the sheriff yesterday turn out to belong to Victor Wolfe. Otherwise, there aren't any other suspects." Hearing some noises at the front of the room, England said, "It looks like our chairman is ready to call the meeting to order." With that, he tipped his hat and walked to the back of the room to stand with Carmel's volunteer fire chief.

Nora had met the Commission's chairman, Doctor Alfred Bolton, on several occasions. Gray-haired, bespectacled, and distinguished-looking, he had retired from teaching at the Massachusetts Institute of Technology. She knew that he lived in a large Craftsman-style house on Professors Row, as a portion of Camino Real was known. She appreciated the fact that he didn't tire an audience with longwinded lectures, the sad habit of many of her former professors at Mills College. Rather, he treated all applicants with respect and listened to their ideas. He made sure they kept to the Planning Commission's schedule and stayed on topic.

For the next hour and a half, Nora took notes on each application, including the one item about numbering the city's residential housing stock. To nobody's surprise, the Commissioners unanimously rejected Fire Chief Nichols' request.

By four o'clock, after completing all of the agenda items, Commissioner Susan Porter, a woman with an extensive background in fine arts, raised her hand. "I want to compliment you, Chairman Bolton," she said. "You've run an efficient meeting. I only hope your discretionary item today is going to be a brief one."

"I echo the sentiments of my fellow Commissioner," said Jessie Botke, an artist from whom Nora had taken a drawing course last summer at the Arts and Crafts Club. "My husband, Cornelius, and I are looking forward to enjoying an early picnic on the beach," she added.

The women's remarks didn't surprise Nora. The Commissioners were volunteers who dedicated themselves to conducting the city's business without compensation.

"Thank you for those kind words, ladies," Chairman Burton said. "However, I'm compelled to ask for your indulgence, since my discretionary item will take some time. Before I get to that, I would like to say how upset the Arts and Crafts Club's membership is about the tragic death of a young actor this past weekend. Although I didn't know Guy Porter personally, I want to extend my sympathies to his family and friends. His killer must be brought to justice. The village's reputation as a theater destination is at stake. This brings me to my topic for today. It concerns the future of theater in Carmel." Raising his voice, he said, "Please come forward, Mr. Preston."

A surprised Nora turned her head to watch Lee walk down the center aisle. Nattily dressed in a double-breasted dark suit, white shirt and tie, he went up to the front table and shook hands with each Commissioner. She blushed when he looked at her and waved, before going over to stand behind the speaker's podium. Why was he here at the Commission's meeting this afternoon, she wondered?

"Is Mr. Kuster joining you today?" the chairman asked.

"No, sir, he isn't," Lee replied. "Mr. Kuster was sorry that he couldn't be with us. He had a prior commitment in San Francisco this afternoon."

Nora was puzzled. She had seen Edward Kuster talking to Lee at the dedication of Father Serra's new statue on Sunday, but he hadn't mentioned what they discussed. She had assumed the director was giving Lee some expert advice on his children's play.

"Then are you prepared to lay out Mr. Kuster's proposal for an indoor theater on Ocean Avenue?"

"Yes, I am, Doctor Bolton."

Now Nora was thoroughly perplexed. She had often heard her boss editorialize about the need for another theater venue in

Carmel, but she didn't know whether Mr. Owens would support constructing a new theater in the middle of a thriving business district. Even more shocking, how had Lee suddenly become involved with Edward Kuster's theater plans?

Her thoughts were interrupted by the chairman's next words.

"How many of you in the audience want to comment on this topic?" Doctor Bolton asked.

Nora watched half a dozen people put up their hands, including the Board of Trustees' new President, Perry Newberry. Apparently, quite a few individuals having an interest in the subject of a new theater had been notified by the Commission's chairman, Nora concluded.

Bolton pointed to Lee. "All right, young man, please begin."

"Thank you, sir," Lee said. "Although I'm a newcomer, I'm aware that the outdoor Forest Theater, and the Arts and Crafts Club's proposed indoor theater on the property it owns, are both located in residential neighborhoods. By contrast, Edward Kuster's proposed theater project is going to be constructed in the center of town. It's fully funded and ready to build immediately. I've brought some preliminary plans of the new indoor theater to share with you and your Commissioners, Chairman Bolton."

Nora heard loud murmurs of disapproval. This was going to be a contentious discussion. In light of that, any plans for Cornelius and Jessie Botke's picnic on Carmel beach would have to be cancelled, she thought.

CHAPTER FIFTEEN

A fter the two women Planning Commissioners on each side of Doctor Bolton leaned over and whispered something, he nodded and said, "We're taking a short break."

Nora appreciated the brief respite. Her hand was tired from all the note taking. She stood up to walk around the room and noticed that the marshal had disappeared. She assumed that Gus Englund had returned to his downstairs office to check his messages and attend to more urgent police business.

Ten minutes later, Chairman Bolton pounded his gavel and said, "Let's call this meeting to order and get started."

It surprised Nora when the Commissioners didn't resume their usual seats. Instead, the five as a group pushed their chairs backwards and spread out to stand behind the front table.

Rapping his gavel again, the chairman said, "We want the audience to come up and join us, so everyone can look at the plans that Mr. Preston is submitting on Edward Kuster's behalf. Before we get to the public comments, however, let me say that we just took an advisory vote. This project will be handled informally for discussion only. The Planning Commission will not be taking any official action today."

Nora picked up her notepad and purse and approached the

front table with the rest of the crowd.

Planning Commissioner Tom Reardon, owner of a plumbing and electrical contracting business in town, smiled as she came up to stand across from him. "I'm sure you'll have plenty to write about when this meeting's over with, miss," he said. "The idea of another theater will be surprising news to Carmel's residents."

"That's right, Mr. Reardon. I plan to record everyone's opinion," Nora said.

Standing across the table from Doctor Bolton, Lee Preston raised his hand and said, "Mr. Chairman, if I might have everyone's attention, please."

Bolton rapped his gavel. "Mr. Preston has the floor."

"Thank you, sir. The first thing I want to point out on these plans is that the project will seat 400 theatergoers"

A murmur rose from the crowd. Nora even saw some heads shaking.

"Also, there will be a separate concert room and studio apartments above the theater," Lee continued, "and commercial shops adjacent to it. I might also add that this could be an ideal venue for showing movies."

The chairman interrupted, "Tell us why we should trust Edward Kuster with such a complex project, Mr. Preston."

"Good question. In addition to his attorney's background, Mr. Kuster is very knowledgeable in the theater business. He has spent years training, both here and abroad, to become an actor, play director, musical composer and set designer. Carmel can do no better than to enthusiastically support his professional vision for a first-class indoor theater in the heart of the village."

"I'm not sure we need it," a voice called out from the other end of the table.

Nora recognized the young man who had spoken. Fair-haired, tall, and lanky, Stephen Pringle was a respected scientist at the Coastal Laboratory run by the Carnegie Institute. An activist and former member of the Board of Trustees, he regularly spoke out on any new building proposals.

"I've performed in plays at the Carmel Club of Arts and Crafts," he began. "Last March, after the successful run of five one-act plays, many of us realized that we needed a larger indoor space with an appropriate stage. The club is now intent on constructing a playhouse on the property and wants to hire M. J. Murphy to come up with plans to build a new theater. I feel compelled to say that Mr. Kuster's proposal sounds like an edifice to someone's ego. Moreover, it would be competing with our playhouse. Who's going to fill his 400 seat theater with only 600 residents in town?"

Nora took down Pringle's words verbatim. His comments would make a perfect sidebar to her story.

"Keep your words less negative, would you, Stephen?" the chairman admonished.

Nodding, Pringle pointed to one of the larger drawings spread out on the table.

"With all due respect, Mr. Chairman, look here. Kuster's stage will be long and extra wide. I understand that he's negotiating to purchase the vacant property across Ocean Avenue from the Pine Inn. That means the theater would dominate the entire block on the south side between Dolores and Monte Verde Streets. And this proposed design doesn't appear to compliment the other buildings that are nearby."

"Are you talking about those old false front buildings that should be torn down anyway?" someone said.

Everyone laughed, releasing some of the tension.

"I would like to speak to your opinion, Stephen," said a soft voice to Nora's right.

It was Charles Sumner Greene. He was a short man in his early 50s, with glasses and graying hair parted in the middle. Despite a nervous habit of clearing his throat several times before speaking, he was a respected Planning Commissioner. Nora knew his views concerning the proposed theater's design would carry weight with others. With his younger brother, Greene had a successful architectural practice in Southern California until retiring to Carmel six years ago. Almost as if everyone around the table shared her thoughts, the group crowded closer together to hear Greene's words.

Pointing to a sketch on the table, he said, "What I find remarkable about Kuster's plan is its emphasis on classic Gothic style. The theater's exterior has a simple, uncluttered appearance. This indicates to me that Mr. Kuster appreciates European architecture. The building, which he plans to call the Carmel Theatre at the Court of the Golden Bough, will change the look of Ocean Avenue and be an asset to the village."

"Thank you for those kind words, sir," Lee interjected. "We all know that theaters are expensive projects. Mr. and Mrs. Kuster plan to spend about $50,000 on theirs, and they have the funds. With no offense meant, I wonder if the Carmel Club of Arts and Crafts does."

Pringle raised his hand. "We do have some seed money, but we're raising more by selling shares to our members and the public at ten dollars each." His face reddened as he raised his voice, "Notwithstanding Mr. Preston's insinuations, the Club is determined to build, even if we need to get a bank loan."

"Competition always makes the product better," Lee responded in a calm voice. "I have something unique to show all of you," he added. Uncovering two sheets of plans that had been buried beneath the others, he spoke directly to Greene. "This is a design for a movable sky-dome. It's clever, don't you think? By providing natural light, as well as fresh air, Mr. Kuster's indoor theater doesn't need to depend on the use of elaborate back drops and lighting for the outdoor scenes."

"It's a novel idea," Greene said, "as long as it doesn't prove too heavy to open."

"May I take a closer look at that sheet?" Perry Newberry asked. The current President of Carmel's elected Board of Trustees stepped around the table to take a position next to Lee. "As a play director, I agree that Mr. Kuster's proposed project has endless possibilities for all types of plays, but I'm also a strong supporter of the Arts and Crafts Club's theater project too." Turning to another man who was standing at the far end of the table, he added, "What do you think, Bert?"

Herbert Heron, the founder of the Forest Theater, had arrived during the Planning Commission's break. He didn't immediately respond to his friend's query. He stroked his chin and said, "I agree with Mr. Greene that the overall design for the theater is quite attractive. But I'm also concerned about the long term effects that Mr. Kuster's project will have on the success of the Arts and Crafts Club's proposed Little Theater, as Stephen Pringle has mentioned. The Club's project, like Kuster's, offers additional indoor space. While it's considerably smaller than what Mr. Kuster is proposing, some may feel that it's all that Carmel needs at this point in time."

"I second that opinion," James Carpenter said. "My group, the Western Drama Society, fully supports the Arts and Craft's Club's theater and will help raise funds for it. Together with our outdoor Forest Theater, I see no need for another theater, especially one in the commercial district that would deprive businessmen of potential retail space."

Nora wondered if Carpenter was being sincere, or if he was harboring a grudge against Lee for having supplanted his canceled play, "A Shadow Falls on Justice."

For the next hour, Nora jotted down phrases, both for and against the project, from several other speakers. She took note of the fact that no Planning Commissioner other than Greene had ventured an opinion. Finally, to her relief, Chairman Bolton said,

"I'm going to poll the Commission. By a show of hands, who would like Edward Kuster's preliminary theater proposal to be continued to a future date unspecified? Say, sometime in the fall, when we will agendize it for a scheduled public hearing?"

Nora saw all Commissioners' hands go up. At the same time, she noticed the disappointed look on Lee's face. He probably expected, at a minimum, some favorable comments from a few of them.

"I'm frustrated with what I've heard," Lee said to the chairman, as he picked up the plans and stepped away from the table. "The least you people could have done is to place this proposed theater on your next scheduled meeting. That way, it could move forward to the Board of Trustees in a timely manner."

"I'm glad they didn't, Preston," James Carpenter said. "I'll do everything in my power to stop it whenever it comes up," the director added, as he brushed past Lee on his way out of the room.

Gathering up her things, Nora felt a light touch on her shoulder. She turned to see Lee standing next to her. "Are you free tonight, Nora?" he asked. "My play auditions are coming up tomorrow night and I want to share some of my ideas with you."

"I'm sorry, Lee, but I have a prior engagement. A good friend is here from San Francisco. She gets to Carmel so infrequently. I'm having dinner with her."

Lee smiled. "I guess I should be glad that it's a woman, and not some suitor."

"Hope I'm not interrupting anything," Perry Newberry said, as he joined them. "I'd like to speak to you in private, Mr. Preston. Do you have a minute?"

"Mr. Preston can have your full attention, Perry." Nora said. "I'm going back to the newspaper office."

"Tell your boss that I'll keep my letters to the editor coming," he countered.

"I'll do that," Nora replied with a grin. She remembered how critical Newberry had been of James Carpenter's hiring of the dead actor, Guy Porter, a Carmel outsider. Most likely, he wanted to caution Lee about doing the same thing. She waved and headed downstairs to the city's offices.

When she reached the closed door with Gus Englund's name on it, she knocked.

"Come on in," the marshal said in a loud voice.

"It's Nora Finnegan," she said, as she entered.

The young man seated in front of Englund's desk jumped up when she saw her.

"Hi, Nora," Tommy Anderson said, as he put on his cap. "I was just leaving. I'm on my way to check if Burt Erickson needs anything while he's on the mend."

"Say hello for me, will you?" Nora said, as she stepped out of his way.

"Shut the door behind you, Tommy. Take a seat, Miss Finnegan. I have news."

"Does this have anything to do with Guy Porter's murder?"

Englund nodded. "Unfortunately, yes. Tommy's in a heap of trouble."

"What has he done?"

Holding out a five dollar bill, Englund continued, "The boy's trying to do the right thing, but he has an uncanny ability of doing it his way — always has. Which isn't necessarily the right way."

"Tommy hasn't had much of an education, Marshal. After his father died in the war in France, he had to drop out of school to support his mother."

"I know all that. That's why I'm not going to charge him for lying to me earlier. Tommy's agreed to return this money to the person who hired him to loosen that piece of scenery behind Guy Porter's sofa last Friday night — the one that luckily missed him."

Nora was stunned. "Who would hire Tommy to do such a thing?"

"The same person who's sitting in jail right now. Victor Wolfe. The five dollar bill is one more piece of evidence pointing to Wolfe as Porter's murderer. Tommy has agreed to testify against him in exchange for giving the boy immunity from jail time."

Nora frowned. "Apparently Victor was doing everything he could to get rid of Guy, so he could replace him in the leading man's role."

"That's his motive," Englund said. "His prints on the milk bottle you found will seal the case against him."

CHAPTER SIXTEEN

Until now, Nora had never had an opportunity to visit Asilomar, the YWCA's conference center occupying sixty oceanfront acres north of Carmel in Pacific Grove. From her vantage point in the back seat of Julia's chauffeured sedan, she glanced at the prominent stone gateposts marking the compound's main entrance. In the dappled light of early evening, she admired the Craftsman-style, Julia Morgan-designed buildings that were scattered among the tall redwoods and Monterey pines. The attractive wood and stone structures seemed to blend into this forest setting, she thought.

Her driver had been instructed to bring her to the Administration Building where Julia would be waiting. Exiting the automobile and stepping inside, Nora was delighted with her surroundings. She paused to peer up at the room's high ceiling with its exposed roof-supporting timbers and appreciated the fact that the redwood walls had been left unpainted in their natural state. Nora could see the beach through a bank of oversized windows running along the far wall. Not surprisingly, in buildings sited along the coastline, where cooling ocean breezes lowered summer temperatures in the evenings, a fire burned in an enormous floor-to-ceiling fieldstone fireplace dominating the middle of the room. Filling one corner by the reception area sat a black grand piano. All the upholstered chairs in the large, rectangular space were empty. Nora assumed that everyone was having dinner — except for the person she had come to meet.

Dressed in her standard black business suit, white blouse and scarf, Julia was seated at an oak desk. She was studying architectural drawings spread out in front of her.

"Hello, Julia," Nora said.

Looking up through round wire-rimmed glasses, the small, dark-haired, middle-aged woman jumped up and gave her young friend a hug. "It's wonderful to be with you again, Nora," she said.

"I'm so happy to see you too." Nora pointed at the architect's plans. "Is that a new project you're designing for this location?"

"Yes, it's called the Tide Inn and its purpose is to house the male employees who work here. In keeping with Mrs. Hearst's plans for Asilomar, the building should be ready for occupancy early next year."

"I remember your telling me that Phoebe Apperson Hearst was influential in helping you get your career started years ago."

"Mrs. Hearst is my patron saint. Through her, I met her son. As you know, William Randolph Hearst commissioned me to design a residence for him down the coast at San Simeon."

Collecting her drawings, Julia led Nora over to a door on the west side of the room. "The dining hall is across the way. I'll tell you more about Asilomar as we walk."

A brisk breeze greeted them as they stepped off the back porch and onto a wide path that snaked from one building to another. Pulling the lapels of her jacket up around her neck, Julia said, "It's colder than usual this evening. I'm pleased to see that you dressed warmly, Nora."

"Living near the ocean, I expect to. I wore this loose-fitting shirt dress to work, but I brought along a heavy sweater for this evening."

"You're a very fashion-sensitive, modern woman, more so than I am, even though I studied in Paris. I think it's wonderful that the new feminine clothing, inspired by French designers like Coco Chanel, allow women more freedom of movement."

"I would never have worn one of those restricting corsets that the women were forced to wear in the pre-war period!"

Chuckling, Julia took Nora's arm. "I'm much older than you, and I managed to avoid squeezing into one of those harnesses. I prefer tailored suits myself. Oh, that's the chapel over there," she added, pointing to her right.

Set amidst the sand dunes, the weathered, shingled building, surrounded by low bushes, looked more like a grand cottage than a traditional, steepled church, Nora thought. "It certainly fits into this landscape well."

"Like the Administration Building, the chapel has a stone fireplace to warm the interior. Although the YWCA primarily uses it for religious services, it can function as an auditorium — even a music hall. I designed the altar space to serve as a stage for the girls' amateur theatrics."

They had come to a low sign on the path that read: Crocker Dining Hall. Ahead of them was a one-story wood building with a very high roof. On entering, Nora was immediately struck by the immense size of the exposed roof trusses overhead. Bentwood cane chairs encircled the dining tables that filled the dining room's cavernous interior. Nora enjoyed seeing groups of chattering girls who were finishing their meals and regaling one another with the day's experiences. They reminded her of her own carefree younger days. A waitress greeted them and showed her and Julia to a table by the window where a reserved sign had been placed on the tabletop. It was already set with placemats, cutlery, and white china coffee cups that were turned over in their matching saucers. Simple elegance, Nora thought.

"Once we finish eating, I'll introduce you to the young lady I spoke about on the telephone," Julia said. "She's waiting for us in the chapel. It's better to meet her there than at her tent house, since there isn't one shred of privacy in those places."

"I saw the tent accommodations on the way in tonight," Nora said. "Those tall, open sheds with striped curtains covering all sides really stand out."

"Yes, they fill a present need. Mrs. Hearst had them delivered here from her home in Pleasanton, where she used them only once for temporary housing at a YWCA gathering. They're quite practical and rainproof. They sit on a raised wood platform and easily shelter a dozen female campers in beds aligned dormitory-style."

"They remind me a bit of army barracks."

"Imagine all the talking that goes on in them before bedtime."

"Talking about all this makes me yearn to be a YWCA girl again," Nora said.

"That tells me you must have a camper's appetite. Let's order our dinner."

Julia unfolded her napkin and placed it on her lap. "The cooks here give the girls plenty of nourishing food while they're away from home. Mrs. Hearst contends that a full tummy helps to ward off all thoughts of homesickness."

"Now I know why I came home from camping weighing ten pounds more."

But tonight Nora wasn't worried about watching her waistline. Mingled with small talk, she enjoyed the three-course meal of soup, salad, and baked snapper, accompanied by generous helpings of mashed potatoes, peas and carrots. When she finished, she was glad that she wasn't wearing a corset.

"Would you like some dessert?" Julia asked.

"No thanks, but I do want to thank you for treating me to supper, and I'm eager to learn more about your mysterious young lady and the problem that needs solving."

Settling into her chair, Julia said, "Her name is Renee Lucien. She is seventeen, and I've known her since birth. She's the granddaughter of an old friend whom I met while studying at the *Ecole des Beaux Arts* in Paris. Renee's parents reluctantly allowed their only daughter to leave home, sail across the ocean, and travel across the country by herself, to spend the summer with her grandfather, my friend, Jean Pierre Lucien. He's the consul general in San Francisco. She has been staying with him at the consulate until she returns home for college. It was I who suggested that she might like to experience the final weeks of her summer here at the YWCA encampment. Therefore, I bear some responsibility for what happened to her this past weekend."

"I'm eager to meet her, and to help you in any way that I can," Nora said.

"We can do that in a few minutes. When I spoke to Renee earlier, she told me she would be attending a movie being shown at the chapel after dinner. It should be over by now. I asked her to sit near the back and wait for us there. Shall we go?"

Although it was almost nine o'clock, there was enough light for the two women to cross the campgrounds to the chapel. When they reached the front door, Nora could hear the sound of a piano playing dramatic music.

"Renee was ecstatic about seeing a cowboy and Indian film tonight," Julia said. "Wait here for me." She opened the door and slipped inside.

A few moments later, Julia and a petite, curvaceous brunette came outside. Whispering something to the girl, and signaling to Nora to follow them, she led the way back to a now empty dining hall and the nearest table that was already set for breakfast.

"We'll have more privacy here," Julia said, and motioned

the two of them to sit with her.

"*Bonsoir,* Miss Finnegan," Renee said, as she took the chair next to Nora. "I love it here in America. Are you really a journalist as my Aunt Julia says?"

Nora noticed that despite Renee's accent, she spoke English very well.

"And did you once live in San Francisco before moving to the Monterey coast?" the girl continued. "You must have many amazing adventures as a reporter. It's such an exciting career for a woman. As for me, I want to be an actress," she said, breathlessly.

"Remember to speak more slowly, dear," Julia cautioned.

The girl's inquisitiveness instantly charmed Nora. She said, "I'm afraid my life isn't as thrilling as you might think, Renee. But how about you? Your aunt Julia has told me that you have a serious problem."

The joy that had been so evident on the girl's pretty face suddenly disappeared. Folding her arms on top of the table, she put her head down and began to cry.

Nora guessed that Renee had nervously been trying to put up a brave front. Leaning over, she patted her arm. "Tell me about it. What's bothering you?"

Looking up, Renee wiped her eyes on the sleeve of her cotton jacket. "Please help me, Nora. If you can't, I will surely die."

"Stop that foolish talk immediately, Renee Marie," Julia said. "You're play-acting again. Nora doesn't work miracles, but, as a journalist in this area, she has her sources, and might be able to help you. Now tell her what you told me, and let's hope she can work things out so you can face your grandfather with a clear conscience."

Renee wiped a tear from her cheek. "All right, *ma tante.* You know best. But first may we have some dessert? It will take away my sadness."

Sighing, Julia summoned a cook who was leaving the dining

room and ready to go home. "Can you bring us some dessert, please?" she asked.

"Of course, Miss Morgan. Right away."

In a few minutes he returned with three servings of strawberry pie and a pot of hot coffee. Julia poured herself a cup. The two young women reached for the wedges of pie.

Nora thought this was an opportunity to cheer up the girl. "Renee, we have an old custom here about eating pie," she said. "Before you start, you cut off the tip of the wedge, set it aside, and make a wish. You then eat the rest of the pie and leave the tip for the last bite. That will make your wish come true."

Renee giggled. *"C'est magnifique,* Nora. You are, how do you say, a lifesaver. I know what to wish for." Closing her eyes, she took several deep breaths.

"It's time for you to start telling all," Julia said sternly, as she sipped her coffee.

Nora had no idea what she was getting into, nor what Renee was about to reveal, but she knew that she had started to bond with a frightened young French girl.

When Renee had finished her story, Julia said, "My car and driver are at your disposal for the rest of the evening, Nora. I sincerely hope you will use the utmost discretion to protect not only Renee's reputation, but the good name of Asilomar and the YWCA."

CHAPTER SEVENTEEN

If Nora had felt nervous tension building inside her while she listened to Renee Lucien talk to her at Asilomar, it couldn't begin to compare to the level of anxiety she was experiencing as Julia's sedan pulled up in front of Sheriff Connery's cottage on Fountain Avenue in downtown Pacific Grove. It was around ten o'clock, and fortunately, the lights in Jimmy's house were on. She was glad that he was still up.

"Marvin's gas station is around the corner," Julia's driver said. "It stays open till eleven, miss. I'll go there from here, get a cold drink, and come back in twenty minutes."

"Thank you, Rodney, but it might take a bit longer to say what I have to say."

He smiled at her. "All you have to do is wave me on if you're not finished talking when I drive by again. I'll go back to the garage for another twenty minutes."

"That sounds like a perfect plan," Nora replied. Pulling her sweater around her shoulders, she stepped out of the automobile. As she walked up the path and approached the cottage, she saw Jimmy and stopped in her tracks. He was sitting on a bench in the dark, on his front porch. Gone were the trappings of his new position. No sheriff's uniform. No black Stetson. No shiny badge and holstered gun. He was wearing a pair of dungarees and a plaid shirt that had seen better days. Nora took a deep breath and opened the fence gate. "Hello, Sheriff," she called out.

"Nora? What are you doing here?" he said, as she stepped up onto the porch.

"I'm sorry to bother you so late at night, but I have news that can't wait until morning. I was in the neighborhood and ... ."

"I know," he interrupted. "You need a ride home." He stood up. "And who was that man who dropped you off just now? I didn't recognize the car when it pulled up. Why are so many men driving you around lately?"

"That doesn't require an answer, and I don't need a ride home. I've come here on business. I want you to listen to what I have to say, Jimmy, because it affects your murder case against Victor Wolfe."

"There's nothing that you can add to it. Both Marshal Englund and I concur that Wolfe killed Guy Porter. He has no alibi for his whereabouts at the time of Porter's death, and he had a strong motive, the means, and the opportunity. The county district attorney is preparing to charge him with homicide."

"Well, you had better rethink that, Sheriff Connery. May I sit down?"

"Sit here next to me and forget that Sheriff bit. You know me better than that."

He pushed aside a pile of laundry and said, "My ma does the washing for Molly and me, but she refuses to fold it."

Nora smiled at his complaint of forced domesticity, but she knew he was making a good home for his six-year-old, motherless daughter. "You're lucky Mrs. Connery lives right next door, Jimmy. She's a big help to you."

"Yes, I know she is. Now would you explain why you've come to see me all the way from Carmel?"

"Actually, I was just at Asilomar, where I had dinner with

my friend, Julia Morgan. She introduced me to a young woman who has some very important information concerning Guy Porter's death. She's a seventeen-year-old French citizen named Renee Lucien."

"What's a French girl doing at Asilomar? More to the point, why would she be interested in a murder case?"

"Let me give you a little background first. I found out that the girl's grandfather is the head of the French consulate in San Francisco. He allowed her to come to the YWCA camp here in Pacific Grove to experience an American tradition firsthand. Renee told me tonight that she and Victor Wolfe are acquainted."

"What's so important about that? What was Wolfe doing at Asilomar?"

"Miss Lucien has a role in a play that's being put on at the campgrounds this summer. It's part of an amateur theatrics program. Apparently, the YWCA hired Victor part-time to teach the girls voice and acting techniques. Renee said that she and Victor were mutually attracted. They've been seeing each other for the past two weeks."

"I'm guessing this Renee person is going to give our killer an alibi for early Saturday morning, at the time that Guy Porter was murdered. Is that it?"

Nora nodded. "You're very perceptive, Sheriff. Yes, Renee admitted to me that she sneaked away from her tent house late Friday night. She and Victor had pre-arranged to meet on the beach at Lovers' Point. They then spent the entire night together. Renee said that the other girls in her tent covered for her at bed-check and until she returned the following morning for breakfast call at eight o'clock."

Connery rubbed his forehead. "Will she step forward and tell her story to me and a judge?"

"She's a minor, Jimmy. Despite her behavior, she must be given anonymity, or she won't talk to you or anybody else."

"Are you asking me to take her statement on your hearsay, so she can keep her identity private, Nora? I'm not going to do that. I can easily subpoena her."

"I don't know whether you can, and she won't talk to you if you do. Her grandfather, the consul general, would intervene to protect her. More than likely, Renee has immunity from American laws. Besides, there's no need to ruin a young woman's reputation and send her home to France disgraced."

"So Victor Wolfe has an alibi. Tell me. How did she learn he was in jail?"

"When you and Deputy Jensen showed up at the Forest Theater Saturday night to arrest him, Victor somehow managed to alert Tommy, the stagehand. He asked him to telephone Renee and let her know that he couldn't make their rendezvous that night because you were taking him in for questioning at the jail in Monterey."

"So by Wolfe not telling me about her, he was protecting this girl from scandal. I've got to hand it to him. There might be some good in him."

"He may be a cad, Jimmy, but he's innocent of murder. He didn't kill Guy Porter. Just because Lee Preston saw Victor walk onstage and take a drink from a cream pitcher that later had acid in it doesn't mean that Victor put the acid in it. That's all conjecture on your part. A good defense attorney will easily dispose of that reasoning. By the way, did you discover Victor's fingerprints on the milk bottle we found in the bushes at the Forest Theater? That would be an important piece of evidence."

"I don't have the results yet. We're shorthanded at the jail, so we've sent Wolfe's prints up to Oakland for identification. But I still think the man has a strong motive, Nora. He wanted to get rid of his rival and take over the leading man's role in your play. I know that's true, because the stagehand Tommy confessed his involvement to Marshal Englund. I have the five dollar bill Victor paid him to loosen up that backdrop on the stage."

"That by itself doesn't make Victor a murderer. Renee's statement that he was with her late Friday night and into the next morning, absolves Victor."

"I can still hold him for intent to harm Porter by paying off the stagehand. I'll notify the district attorney to hold off on the murder charge on Wolfe until I interview the girl."

"One more thing. Renee will only agree to talk to you if you don't reveal her identity. I want you to promise that you will do that."

"As you said, she is a minor. I have to legally abide by that and keep her name from becoming public."

"That's good. She's a vulnerable young woman who made an impulsive decision to get involved with a man she hardly knew. I believe she's learned a painful lesson."

Jimmy nodded. "We'll call her Jane Doe. The judge will accept that. I'll see the young lady tomorrow morning and get her tent mates to corroborate her story."

He remained silent for a moment, and then said, "I'll drive you home to Carmel tonight. My parents will watch over Molly for me until I get back."

His words surprised her. "You're mixing up things that have no relationship to one another, Jimmy."

Reaching out, he touched her face and put his arms around her.

Nora felt the heat of his body against hers and recalled the attraction as when they first fell in love last winter. His next move was unexpected, but she didn't turn her face to avoid his kiss.

Remembering that she had come here tonight to fulfill a promise to another young woman, she knew how emotions affect decisions. "We'll need to make a short stop at Marvin's gas station before we go on to Carmel."

He raised his eyebrows. "You don't have to pay for gasoline,

Nora. It's my treat."

Laughing, she nudged his forearm. "I'll explain it to you on the way, Jimmy. Let's go."

CHAPTER EIGHTEEN

Wednesday

S tifling a yawn, Nora entered the newspaper office and greeted Mr. Owens. He was behind the reception counter, already assembling copies of the latest issue of the *Carmel Pine Cone* for Tommy Anderson to distribute. Dasher, the Owens' Welsh corgi, lay near the open front door, basking in the morning sun.

On the way to her desk, Nora leaned down and patted the distinctive white blaze on the little dog's sable-colored head. Removing her hat, she fluffed her short black curls with her fingers and dropped her purse in her desk's bottom drawer. She rejoined Mr. Owens at the front counter.

Glancing over at her, he smiled and said, "I'm picking Mrs. Owens and Sally up at the railroad station today, Honora. I'd like you to take charge of things while I'm gone — and that includes supervising Dasher." Pointing his finger at the dog, he continued, "Make sure he doesn't sneak off into the back room again and chew on things."

Dasher raised his head and barked, as if to object to his master's remark.

"Your family will be glad to be home, after a long, tiring

train ride." Cutting a piece of twine, Nora handed it to him to tie a bundle of newspapers together. She too would be happy to have Mary Lee Owens back at work. Not only had she assumed the receptionist's duties these past weeks, but she had ignored for the most part Mr. Owens' officious moods, something that his wife didn't tolerate. "By the way," she said, "while you're out of the office, I'll be working on an important piece of information in the Guy Porter murder case."

"Has there been a breakthrough?"

"Yes. You remember the San Francisco architect, Julia Morgan? She asked me to talk to a young woman who is claiming that Victor Wolfe was nowhere near the scene of the crime when Guy Porter was murdered last weekend."

"I'm very impressed by the contacts you've developed since I hired you last year, Honora. Go on."

Nora explained about Renee Lucien. "She's a minor, Mr. Owens. However, when she heard about Victor's arrest, she couldn't remain silent and see an innocent man convicted of murder. The sheriff is honoring her anonymity and I'll keep the girl's name out of my article."

"She's very brave to admit to an indiscretion and you played an important role in getting her confession. Leave your story on my desk when you're finished. I'll run it in the next issue."

Returning to her desk, Nora removed her typewriter cover, but before she could start typing, the telephone rang. She picked it up and said, "*Carmel Pine Cone*. How may I help you?"

"It's Keith, Nora. I'm calling to see if you'll have lunch with me today. Say one o'clock? That's when my library volunteer comes in to relieve me."

"I would love to, but only if you bring sandwiches and root beer here to the *Pine Cone*. I'm stuck on desk duty all day. Can you tell me what's on your mind?"

"I'd rather discuss it with you in person," he said in a

brusque voice. "See you there at one." He hung up.

Her friend's abruptness meant only one thing. He had woman trouble. Keith always used Nora as a sounding board. She guessed he had been rebuffed once again by a sometime girlfriend. She would look forward to his news. It would break up her day.

Turning the front window sign from 'Open' to 'Closed,' Nora greeted Keith and showed him into Mr. Owens' empty office. After collecting two water glasses from the supply closet, she shut the door behind her to keep Dasher out. Clearing space on the publisher's messy desk, she said, "You sounded upset on the telephone. What's wrong?"

He dragged up a chair, but didn't answer. Taking the sandwiches out of a brown paper bag, he put them on the desk. "I thought maybe biting into a dill pickle would make me feel better," he said. Dipping into the bag again, he brought out two smelly ones. "I picked these out of the barrel myself. They're Leidig's best-sellers."

Nora frowned. "You can have mine. Those pickles match your sour disposition." She sat down and poured some root beer from an amber-colored bottle into their glasses.

Leaning back in his chair, Keith began crunching on a pickle.

After listening to him chew away his pent-up irritation, Nora took her roast beef sandwich out of its wrapping. "All right, Mr. Preston, I've given you enough time to put together a few sentences that will help me understand your latest troubles."

Wiping his mouth with his handkerchief, Keith shook his head. "I just can't believe this is happening. After I came home from the library yesterday, my father telephoned me all the way from Charleston. He and Mother wanted to make me aware of a serious family matter."

"Is one of them ill?"

"They're fine, but I hope what they're going through doesn't make them sick. This concerns my brother, Lee. Apparently he called and asked them to withdraw a very substantial sum from our trust fund and send the money to him here in Carmel."

"What did he say he was going to do with it?"

"He said it was going to be an investment in his future. But he kept the details non-specific. I don't know what to make of it. Since graduating from college, Lee seems to have done well financially, so why would he need all that money?"

"Have you talked to him about it?"

"I did. He came over to the cabin last night for supper. But he won't explain. He said that the less said about it, the better. That made me worry even more, which is why I had to talk to you. I thought he might have told you something, since the two of you have been keeping company."

"We're hardly doing that." Nora's thoughts flashed back to last night's amorous encounter with Jimmy. "He's a very nice man, but your brother and I aren't involved. We have discussed one topic lately, and that's his desire to help Edward Kuster build an indoor theater here in Carmel. Lee wants me to give the project some favorable publicity in the *Pine Cone* as the public discussion moves ahead. However, there's been no talk of money."

"I hadn't heard about that. All Lee talks about non-stop is the children's play he's putting on at the Forest Theater in October. I don't think he needs any extra money to do that."

"Didn't you encourage him to enter our amateur play competition last spring?"

"Yes, I did, but I didn't think it would spark these kinds of crazy notions. Last night Lee told me he walked out on a lucrative job in Hollywood, to come up here and 'find his passion.' He's not thinking straight."

Putting down her sandwich, Nora decided to probe a little

deeper. "How much money does Lee want from the trust fund?"

"Twenty five thousand dollars. And half of that money belongs to me. It's supposed to pay for the upkeep of our family's plantation that Lee and I will inherit after our parents have passed on. I'm upset, and so are they. It's a lot of money to risk."

"Have they sent it?"

"Not yet." Sitting up in his chair, Keith continued, "I want to get to the bottom of this. Lee told me he has auditions scheduled for the parts in his play tonight. Come to the theater with me, will you? Maybe we'll find out what's going on."

Nora remembered that Jimmy had wanted to see her tonight also, but he had a county supervisors' meeting this evening in Salinas. He had asked her about tomorrow night, but she was reluctant to accept his invitation and start things up again.

"Nora, are you listening to me?"

"Sorry, my mind was elsewhere. I'll be happy to go with you. It might be fun, given all the actors who will probably show up. It also has the potential of being very informative."

He looked relieved. "I knew I could count on you. I'll pick you up after work and we can walk together."

"Have you told anyone else about the money?"

"You're the only one, and I hope you don't tell anyone else — especially not Lee."

"You can trust me," Nora said, and she meant it.

CHAPTER NINETEEN

"I'm pleased that so many of you Carmelites came out tonight," Lee Preston said to the growing crowd. Wearing white linen slacks and a wide-collared shirt with sleeves rolled up to his elbows, he made his way towards the center of the outdoor stage.

Nora and Keith had taken seats in the Forest Theater's top row, where they could observe everything that was happening. Young families with fidgeting children occupied the lower rows. Nora picked out the Jacklin family among them.

"Those who are interested in being interviewed for a part in my play, will you please take seats in the front row," Lee said.

On hearing his request, Claudia, Rob, and Freddie Jacklin stood up and moved down.

Lee continued, "I'll begin auditions for the role of young Jesse Markham, the main character in my children's play, *The Captain and the Caterpillar.*"

Freddie got up and ran over to stand with several boys near the stage.

Lee paused until they quieted down, and then said, "Jesse is a very curious boy with superior intelligence. He has the uncanny ability to predict things before they happen. It's an important role, and somewhat challenging." Turning to address the audience, he said, "Parents, I'll be evaluating your sons carefully, but kindly, especially if I conclude they aren't right for the part."

Listening to his reassuring words, Nora thought that Lee was well-suited to be the author and director of a children's play. He had the patience and the temperment.

Keith nudged her. "Look who's arrived. I wonder why she's decided to come."

"Vera's an aspiring actress, and I think she would want to try out for a role in Lee's play. But what I don't understand is why she's wearing those high-heeled pumps on these uneven dirt paths."

They stopped talking to watch the attractively coiffed and dressed redhead walk gingerly along the front aisle and take a seat in the row behind Claudia and Rob.

Keith snickered. "As always, Vera loves to draw attention to herself. It's not going to do her much good in this case."

"Why do you say that?"

"Because this afternoon my brother told me there was only one female part in his play, and that's the boy's mother. Vera Winfield's hardly the motherly type."

"I disagree, Keith. The stage is a magical place, and if Vera's a good actress, she can always don a gray wig and, with the right makeup, look older than her years. However, my choice for the mother's role would be Claudia Jacklin — that is, if she's here to audition for the part."

"I agree. It would be good for her. Yesterday when she and Freddie visited the library, she told me how disappointed she was not to have the leading role in Carpenter's play. It really upset her when it was suddenly cancelled. I know why she felt that way. All of you cast members had been rehearsing for weeks and weeks."

"It's more than that. Claudia is an artist. She needed that role to nurture her soul. After years of working as a trained photographer, she was devastated when all of her pictures were destroyed in that house fire last fall. She needs a new creative outlet."

Keith nodded. "As an aspiring plein-air artist, I can understand how she feels."

A tall, middle-aged man entered the theater and caught Nora's attention. Coming up the aisle, the actor, Randall King, shook hands with Rob, smiled at Claudia, and took a seat on the wood bench behind the couple and next to Vera.

"There's someone I can see in the role of the captain in Lee's play," Nora said.

"Why don't you go down there and help my brother choose the cast?" Keith took on a serious face, followed by a quick grin. "All kidding aside, you'd be good at it, Nora. Why not try out for a part tonight? You're an aspiring actress just like Vera. Aren't you interested in having Lee pick you?"

Nora laughed. "As you said, there's only one female role. Would you describe me as the motherly type? You know from experience that I can barely cook."

"Don't sell yourself short. I've had some good meals at your place this past year. What about that tuna casserole your family's housekeeper taught you to make before you left home to live on your own?"

"You're so supportive," she said, poking him with her elbow. "Mrs. Simon was absolutely horrified when I told her afterwards why it didn't work out as well as I had hoped. I'd forgotten to boil the noodles first before putting the tuna dish in the oven."

"I thought they were a tad crispy, but they were edible," Keith teased.

Their conversation was interrupted by the sound of footsteps tramping across the stage. Nora watched a group of five boys gather in front of Lee. The playwright, seated on a tall stool, towered above them. She mused that Lee was the *captain*, ready to address his *caterpillars*.

"I'm going to ask each of you to take this page of script and read it out loud," Lee said. Shifting on his stool, he looked out at the audience, and added, "I'll be reading the role of Jesse's father, Captain Billy Markham, a Civil War veteran who, after the conflict ended, left Mississippi and brought his family to settle in California's Central Valley." He gazed down at the boys and said, "Let's begin with you, Freddie Jacklin."

It pleased Nora to hear her young friend's name called out. The boy was the kind of son she hoped she could have one day. As she noticed Freddie look over at his mother before reaching for the paper from Lee, she felt a bit jealous of Claudia, who nodded and waved at the boy. Nora imagined the love in the mother's face as she sent a silent message of encouragement to her son.

"Now, Freddie, I'll cue you in this first scene," Lee said. "That means after I finish talking, you read your words. Just make believe you're talking to your father."

"My real father is dead," Freddie replied, "but I've been adopted by another man who's going to be my dad. Does that count?"

A murmur went through the audience.

Lee smiled. "That couldn't be better, son. You're an actor already." Handing Freddie a sheet of paper, he added, "Let's begin. Remember, I'm Captain Markham and you're my son, Jesse."

Waiting for his cue, Freddie kept his eyes on the script.

CAPTAIN MARKHAM: *(puts down the shovel and wipes his head with a rag)* It's time for you to learn how to farm, Jesse. We're planting a new crop here that is going to feed us all through the winter, son.

JESSE: "Yes, Father. I want to learn. And when we finish here, will you let me drive that old plow you bought from the farmer who sold us this place? *(He picks up the shovel, which is taller than he is, and stabs at the dirt.)*

Nora thought Freddie seemed a bit tentative at first, but to her surprise, he took to his role immediately. He spoke clearly and with the proper emphasis, even as far as lifting an imaginary shovel and driving it down into the soil.

Suddenly, the scene was interrupted by the voices of two men who were striding towards the stage. Lee looked over at them and said, "What's this about? We're in the middle of auditions."

"Why is James Carpenter here with Marshal Englund?" Nora whispered to Keith. The lawman's presence reminded her of the night Gus Englund had interviewed the cast members of Carpenter's play here in this theater. It hadn't been at all pleasant. "Let's get closer," she said. "I want to hear what those men are saying."

Getting up from their seats, the two hurried down to a lower row and settled next to Vera and Randall.

Lee had already jumped off the stage to confront Englund and Carpenter.

"I don't like the looks of this," Keith said, shaking his head.

Nora saw that Herbert Heron had also come down from his seat to join the group.

"I have a Temporary Restraining Order," Carpenter said, as he handed a document to the marshal. "I want you to serve this legal document on Lee Preston and Herbert Heron."

Englund took the paper and said, "Mr. Carpenter's lawyer received this order from Judge Sargent of the Monterey County Superior Court. I'm afraid I have to shut down your play, Mr. Preston. This also countermands Mr. Heron's order to cancel Mr. Carpenter's play until a judge can hear the matter. Consider yourselves served."

"Can't you help me out here, Mr. Heron?" Lee pleaded. "You run this theater."

Heron scanned the order and then looked at Lee. "According to this document, James is entitled to halt any audition, rehearsal, or performance of *The Captain and the Caterpillar*. I'm sorry,

Lee, but the Society is legally required to shut down your play."

"Lee looks very angry," Keith said to Nora. "I hope my brother controls his temper and doesn't do anything stupid." He was relieved when Lee shrugged his shoulders, turned, and walked towards the exit.

"I think we should go talk to your brother before he leaves," Nora said.

They found Lee standing outside the Forest Theater next to his Cadillac. He was about to get into the vehicle.

"I'm terribly sorry this happened," Nora said.

Lee grinned. "I'll get over it, but thanks for your concern. I'm glad to see the two of you. Would you like to go for a drive? I could use some time to cool off." Opening the front passenger's door, he added, "There's a place out in Carmel Valley that serves decent food. And Keith, I hope you won't be too worried if Nora drives us back to Carmel. She's been anxious to take lessons."

"Around here, it would be a curiosity to see a lady driving an automobile," Keith said. "But if any woman can, it's Nora." Looking at her, he added, "We'll have a good time and I'm confident Lee will stake us to our meals on his Hollywood salary."

"Hey! Wait for me!" Vera shouted, as she ran up to join them.

"What kept you?" Lee said.

Vera giggled. "My new shoes may look stylish, but they aren't made for walking." Moving past Nora, she climbed into the back seat with Keith.

Nora's nose picked up the scent of Vera's spicy perfume. It was her way of attracting men, she thought.

"You're impossible, Vera," Lee said, as he helped Nora into the front passenger seat. Leaning in, he whispered, "I'm sorry. I asked her to join me for a ride in the country after auditions were over."

As she listened to Keith babble on about Vera's new shoes,

Nora wondered if she had made a wise decision to go riding with the Preston brothers. However, she did want to learn how to drive.

CHAPTER TWENTY

Leaving the village, Lee took a narrow road going east that followed the course of the river into Carmel Valley. Traffic was light, as they moved at a steady pace past dairy farms, ranches and homesteads that dotted the rural area. Nora had never been out here before, although she had heard wild stories of grizzly bears roaming the surrounding Santa Lucia Mountains. The light had begun to fade and the temperature was dropping.

After a short ride, Lee turned the wheel and pulled the Cadillac into a clearing below a grove of tall eucalyptus trees. Staring out the window, Nora realized this was their destination. She saw several automobiles parked in front of a weathered cabin sited far back from the road. The front windows were covered with burlap, and despite the front door being closed, she heard loud music coming from inside. Someone had chiseled "Egan's" on a wooden sign swaying back and forth at the entrance.

"Quinlan introduced me to this roadhouse, and I've brought Lee here a few times," Keith piped up.

Wrinkling her nose, Nora said, "If you're referring to the owner of the Shamrock Garage on Ocean Avenue, I've heard you say that Pete Quinlan's a bit of a tippler."

"Maybe he is, but I enjoy his company," Keith said, as he

helped Vera out of the back seat. Looking over at his brother, he said, "Why don't we let the two women get us a table and order some food? You and I can go out back and sample the hard cider while the cook fixes our meal."

Lee frowned. "You go ahead. I'll stay with the ladies. Someone has to protect them from the local lads who will accost them just as soon as they walk in."

Keith nodded and disappeared around the side of the cabin.

Holding open the front door, Lee followed Nora and Vera to an unoccupied table in the far corner. The place was dark, noisy and crowded. The music Nora had heard was coming from three musicians seated on a raised platform: a fiddler, a guitar player and a drummer. Each man wore cowboy attire with matching bandannas around their necks.

Almost immediately, a young man in denim work clothes walked up to the table, tipped his Stetson, and asked Vera if she wanted to dance.

She looked at Lee, who nodded. Vera smiled, got up, and accompanied the fellow to an area on the opposite side of the room reserved for dancers.

"Do you feel comfortable here, Nora?" Lee asked. "If not, I'll locate Keith and we'll leave right now."

Nora had never been to a roadhouse before. She wasn't about to let what might be a one- time experience slip away. "I'm perfectly fine," she said. "I like this music, but where did Vera learn that dance step she's doing?"

Lee glanced over at the couple, who, by now, were swaying rhythmically to a fast beat. "I'm betting she picked it up while starring in a musical play she was performing in. She's a good dancer, I'll give her that."

Just then, a young woman with curly black hair like Nora's sashayed up to the table. Her gingham dress had a low cut bosom and rode well above her knee. Smiling at Lee, she said, "I'm

Peggy, your waitress. Are you here to try our cider?" She pointed at the counter stacked with white cups and saucers. "We serve it in those coffee cups. Shall I put you down for two coffees?"

"I don't know what our friends want, but we'll have two sarsaparillas," Lee said.

Nora noticed that several other couples had joined Vera and her partner on the dance floor. She turned back to Lee. "Did Keith and I interrupt what you and Vera had planned tonight?"

"What do you mean?"

"When she came up to us outside the Forest Theater, I heard you say, 'What kept you?' It made me think that you might have arranged to come out here to Egan's and Keith and I butted in."

"That's not the way it was. Vera is out for a good time. I've seen lots of young women like her while working in Hollywood — starlets who are always trying to get their claws into some man. Gold-diggers, I believe they're called."

"I don't think Vera's that kind of girl, Lee. When she moved to Carmel two months ago to be the lead understudy in James Carpenter's play, she quickly found a job at Levy's general store to support herself. She tries to look glamorous and she enjoys flirting, but that doesn't make her a gold-digger."

"You're probably right," Lee said, shrugging his shoulders. "Changing the subject, what's been going on with the Porter murder case? Since the sheriff showed up at the theater the other night and took Victor Wolfe to jail for questioning, I haven't heard a thing."

Nora had no thoughts of betraying her source, the French girl, Renee Lucien, nor would she provide Lee with explicit details. She said, "I understand that a witness has come forward to give Victor an alibi for the time of Guy's death."

"Is he still in jail?"

"Apparently the sheriff is holding him for something else. I plan to speak with him tomorrow and get an update for my follow-up story."

"I've never met a woman who likes working in a male-dominated world as much as you do, Nora. Tell me why you enjoy this investigative reporting." Reaching across the table, he took her hand. "The truth is, I find you fascinating, and I'd like us to become more than just friends."

Drawing her hand back and putting it in her lap, she thought of Jimmy.

Peggy reappeared. The waitress saved Nora from answering. Carrying a tray with a bowl, two bottles and two glasses, she placed it on the table and said, "I brought some roasted peanuts to tide you over while your supper's cooking. Do you want to order? Tonight we have a house special."

"What would that be, miss?" Lee asked.

With a quick smile and a twinkle in her eyes, she said, "It's what we have every night: barbecued beef, baked beans, and cole slaw."

"Sounds delicious. Let's have four orders then."

"Boy, you must be hungry, sir!"

Lee smiled at her. "No. We have two more people who will be joining us."

Half-listening, Nora tapped her foot to the music and watched Vera and the young man dance. However, she was having some difficulty seeing them through the thick cloud of cigarette smoke.

When the waitress returned with their food, she began distributing the plates. "Everything's hot," she said. "Hope your two guests come before the meals cool."

"We might as well start," Lee said. "Who knows when Vera will come back to the table, and Keith is having a good time with his friends outside."

Nora picked up a checkered napkin and placed it in her lap. The food smelled delicious and she was hungry. Turning around to look at the dance floor one last time before she starting eating, she was surprised when she couldn't locate Vera among the fast-moving couples. Her bright yellow peasant skirt and matching off –the-shoulder blouse should have been easy to spot.

Reaching over and tapping Lee's arm, she said, "I know this sounds odd, but I'm worried. Vera's disappeared. Where could she and her partner have gone?"

Lee took a swallow of soda, stood up, and edged over to the dance floor. Seconds later, he returned to the table. "I'm not exactly sure where she is. I'll head outside and check on her. Perhaps she's met up with Keith. I don't want her getting into trouble."

"I'm going with you," Nora said, and followed him. Standing with Lee on the back stoop, she took in the length of the dirt yard and the grove of tall trees that bordered the area. A low shed about the size of a chicken coop had been built between the trees and the roadhouse. In front of it, a dozen or so men loitered around an old wooden barrel sitting on a low table. Keith was among them. Nora saw him bend over, open the spigot at the bottom of the barrel, and fill a Mason jar with a pale liquid. He stepped back and took a long drink.

"Stay here. I'll tell Keith his food is on the table," Lee said. He headed toward his brother.

Looking around, Nora wondered if Vera would be foolish enough to accompany a stranger into that secluded area behind the trees. Their low hanging limbs seemed to interlace and it was difficult to see beyond them. Rather than wait for Lee to return, she decided to begin her own search. Picking her way through the underbrush, her shoes crushed a few pods of eucalyptus. A pungent, mentholated odor drifted upward.

Following a narrow path that someone had improvised, in a few minutes she came upon a dilapidated outbuilding nearly hidden from view. Trying the door, she opened it and stepped inside. When her foot bumped into something, she looked down and saw one of Vera's high-heeled shoes. Squinting into the semi-darkness, Nora followed the outline of a man who was running toward an open door at the rear of the shed.

Startled, she waited a few seconds for her eyes to adjust to the dim lighting. But the man was gone. In the far corner a woman lay on a small cot. It was Vera. Her blouse had slipped off her shoulders and her skirt was rumpled. Red blotches covered her throat. Her eyes were wide open and said it all: stark terror.

"I'll get help," Nora cried out, and ran back to the roadhouse to find Lee and Keith.

CHAPTER TWENTY ONE

As they were about to leave Egan's roadhouse, the waitress came outside. Running up to the Cadillac, Peggy handed a blanket to Vera and said, "Maybe this will keep you warm on the ride home, miss. I'm praying for you."

Tears filled Vera's eyes. Taking the blanket, she said, "Thank you so much."

There was no thought of a driving lesson tonight. Nora asked Keith to move up front with his brother, while she sat with Vera in the back seat. Returning to Carmel along the river road, no one in the automobile spoke. The attack on Vera had cast a pall on Lee's plans to enjoy an evening together. Not even the usually talkative Keith said anything. Smelling his breath, Nora thought he had imbibed one too many "coffees."

When they pulled up in front of the San Carlos Lodge, Nora reached over, expecting to help Vera out. Instead, the young woman threw off the blanket and bolted.

"She seems very upset," Nora said to Lee and Keith. "I'm going to telephone Doctor Barnes and have him come over and take a look at her."

"That's a good idea," Lee said.

"I'll stop by tomorrow and see how she's doing," Keith muttered.

Getting out of the automobile, Nora waved at them as they drove away. She followed Vera into the boarding house.

Annie Stevens was dozing on the sofa in front of the fireplace. A newspaper lay open on her lap. She woke up when she heard the front door close. Seeing Vera being guided by Nora towards the staircase, the landlady stood up and came over to them. "You don't look too good," she said. "What's the matter, Vera?"

"I'll explain it to you later," Vera said in a hoarse voice. "Nora is going to help me up to my room. I want a bath, and after that, I'm going to bed."

Annie gave Nora a puzzled look, as if to say, 'When is someone going to tell me what's going on?'

"Will you make Vera some tea, Annie?" Nora asked. "I'll come get it shortly."

"We could all use some. I'll make a pot."

Upstairs, Nora located Vera's bathrobe and helped her get undressed. She noticed that the bright red splotches on the actress' neck had gotten worse.

"I feel so exhausted," Vera said. "I think I'll rest for a while."

"That's a good idea," Nora replied. And while I'm downstairs getting your tea, I'll ask Annie to telephone Doctor Barnes. You need his help. Not to hurt your feelings, but I can't figure out any good reason why you would go off with that cowboy."

Yawning, Vera stretched out on the bedspread and closed her eyes. "I sure was a fool to listen to Tex, but it got hot out there on the dance floor. When he suggested we take a walk and look at the stars, I just didn't see any harm in it. I knew Keith was out there talking with his friends. I never expected any rough stuff, but the next thing I knew, Tex was dragging me into the shed and pushing me down on that filthy cot."

"Who was he? Did he say he was from around here?"

"He didn't talk much. Besides, I was too busy admiring his good looks to be suspicious."

"If you don't mind my asking you a personal question, were you violated tonight? If you were, you need to tell Sheriff Connery. That kind of assault is a serious crime."

"I wasn't attacked in that way, Nora. Tex, or whoever he was, tried to choke me, not rape me. I'm really frightened. Please stay until the doctor comes."

"I'll stay as long as you need me. I'll go get your tea."

In the kitchen, Nora reassured Annie that Vera had a run-in with a wild cowboy, and would she mind calling Doctor Barnes. She then went upstairs to the bathroom to light the gas under the water coils, and returned to the bedroom. Setting a mug of tea on Vera's nightstand, she said, "While you've been resting, I started heating the water for your bath."

Sitting up, Vera took the mug and sipped the steaming Chamomile. Then, putting the mug down and taking a bath towel, she slipped off the bed and headed out the door to the bathroom down the hall.

Nora sat down on a straight-back chair just as the grandfather clock downstairs struck ten. She was too stimulated to remain seated.

Getting up, she looked around the actress' bedroom. The clothes closet door was wide open. The first thing she noticed was that Vera had grouped her clothing according to the season. Summer wear filled the rack on the left side of the closet, while winter outfits had been placed together on the right. One hanger, covered with a cloth to keep out the dust, held a beautiful silver fox fur. Six pairs of high-heeled pumps formed an orderly line along the floor. Nora decided that Vera was overly extravagant with so many different shoes to choose from.

She stared up at the top shelf and spotted several hatboxes, each embossed with "City of Paris," San Francisco's finest department store. *Vera was a shopper.*

Something caught her attention on the top of the dresser against the back wall. She crossed the room for a closer look. Sitting next to Vera's tortoise shell hairbrush was a small crystal bottle with the word "Chanel" neatly printed in black letters on its white label. She had read about Coco Chanel, the up-and-coming French designer. Apparently the woman sold perfume as well as clothing.

Nora's eyes couldn't avoid scanning the contents of two open dresser drawers. They held folded piles of lacy lingerie, hand-knit sweaters and colorful silk scarves. She wondered how a struggling actress who worked in a Carmel general store had been able to buy so many extravagant things.

Just then, the sound of bare feet slapping on the hallway's floorboards caused her to turn around.

The bedroom door swung open.

"Did you miss me, Nora?" Vera said, as she walked in. "I'm feeling so much better, thanks to that energizing bath."

She did seem more like her old self, Nora thought.

Kneeling down in front of the dresser, Vera opened the bottom drawer and pulled out a faded flannel nightgown. "This belonged to my mother." Looking back at Nora, she added, "When I left home years ago, I took it with me so I could always remember her. If she were still alive, she would be very grateful to you, as I am. You saved my life tonight and you've been so kind to me. I just couldn't tell Annie what I went through at the roadhouse, not until I got control of my emotions."

"That's understandable. You've been through a terrible experience."

They were interrupted by a sharp knock on the bedroom door. A male voice said, "It's Doctor Barnes, Miss Winfield. May I come in?"

Nora went over to the door and opened it. "Hello, Doctor Barnes. I'm not sure if you remember me from the other morning. I'm Nora Finnegan."

"Of course, Miss Finnegan. We were introduced last Saturday when I came to pronounce Guy Porter dead. We seem to meet under strange circumstances, don't we?"

"I guess we do." The smile on Zachary Barnes' face lifted Nora's spirits. She hadn't realized how shocked she had been by Vera's physical ordeal.

"May I come in? I'd like to examine Miss Winfield."

Nora stepped back. "Thank you for coming, Doctor. It's late, and you have a family, but Vera needs those marks on her neck looked at."

"I'm always available to patients. As to your thoughtful reference to my family, I'm afraid I'm all there is. I'm a bachelor."

Embarrassed, Nora said, "I'll be waiting downstairs." She went out into the corridor to give Vera and the doctor some privacy.

When she reached the first floor, she found Annie sitting and talking with a visitor in the lodge's kitchen. Getting up from the table, Annie said, "I'll pour you a nice cup of tea, Nora. Join us. You know James Carpenter."

The director stood up. "Hello, Nora. I just arrived. It's late, but I had to come. It concerns Vera. A short while ago, Claudia Jacklin telephoned me and told me she was quitting our play. I came right over here to offer her part to Vera."

The news surprised Nora. "But isn't your play in limbo until a judge decides whether you can put it on?"

"My lawyer assures me that I have a binding contract with the Forest Theater Society. It can't be broken without my consent. I'm already putting together a new cast, with Vera as the lead female and me in Guy Porter's role of the defense attorney."

Nora shook her head. "I guess we'll just have to see what

the judge has to say."

Carpenter frowned. "By the way, Annie says Vera's had an accident. What happened?"

"It's personal," Nora said. "If she wants to explain it to you, that's up to her."

"James has been very kind to Vera ever since Guy passed on," Annie interjected. "If she were sitting here having tea with us, she would tell you to trust him, Nora. Tell us what happened to her."

Nora wasn't sure that she should. A thought crossed her mind. She recalled something Lee had mentioned. Last April, he had met James Carpenter at the Bohemian Club. A month later, Vera and Guy had come down from San Francisco to act in James' new play. How long had Carpenter known Vera Winfield? Could he have paid for the costly items in Vera's bedroom?

"Tell me what this is all about, Nora," James said. "Should anything bad happen to Vera, it would trouble me immensely."

"I'm afraid you'll have to ask her." Nora stood up and put her teacup in the sink. "I'm going to check on her again before I leave for home."

Climbing the stairs, Nora's mind was racing. She had seen Vera flirting with James during rehearsals. Now the director was offering her the starring role in his play. Guy Porter had also been on the receiving end of Vera's affections, but she had taken up with James immediately after Guy's sudden demise.

What if James Carpenter had seen the younger man as a rival? Jealousy could be a powerful motive.

CHAPTER TWENTY TWO

Thursday

On her way to work the next morning, Nora took a detour past the new building on the west side of Dolores Street near Seventh Avenue. It was moving day for the city's staff. As part of her reporter's job, she always attended Carmel's Planning Commission meetings where, some months before, she had seen a preview of how the new two-story, stucco post office had been designed. Staring up at its bay windows on the upper floor and its Spanish tile roof, she admired the final result. Carmel was very lucky to have the architect, Charles Sumner Greene, as a member of the Commission. He guided the group's decisions by pointing out the merits of good architecture.

Since arriving here from San Francisco last September, Nora had come to accept the modest one-story, wood-framed structures lining both sides of Ocean Avenue, the village's main street. However, the new post office and several other structures being considered for Dolores Street looked far more interesting and permanent to her. Carmel seemed to be in the beginning stages of a building boom.

Passing in front of the post office entrance, she avoided a pair of workmen who were unloading pieces of office furniture.

Nora stepped around them and nearly collided with a grim-faced Marshal Gus Englund. He had come out the side door to watch the movers. It suddenly occurred to her that his office would now be in this building, as part of the relocated City Hall.

"Hello, Miss Finnegan," he grumbled. "I hope your day is starting off better than mine. You wouldn't think this would happen, but on their way from the old City Hall down the street on Ocean Avenue, those two men have misplaced three of my file boxes." Pointing at the moving truck, he added, "They were supposed to be in that load, and they aren't. There will be the devil to pay if they don't find them before my morning meeting with the sheriff."

Why was Jimmy coming to Carmel, Nora wondered? "I wasn't aware that Sheriff Connery would be in town today. I'm puzzled. Do you mind my asking what his business concerns?"

"Always the curious reporter, eh, Miss Finnegan? Well, don't apologize. You're simply doing your job. What I can tell you is that the sheriff received a telephone call from someone out in Carmel Valley last night. It's not my jurisdiction, of course, but there was some kind of an incident at Egan's roadhouse. They've had trouble there from time to time. Apparently some young people from Carmel were involved, and one was assaulted. They left the scene before Egan could get to the bottom of it. The sheriff and I will be driving out there to interview him."

Apparently Egan had called the sheriff. Nora was relieved when the marshal took up another subject.

Pointing at the vacant lot to the north of the post office, Englund said, "I heard that a second building will be going up next door pretty soon."

"I saw the preliminary plans for it at the last Planning Commission meeting. It's also a two-story, stucco building that looks very similar to the one you're moving into, Marshal. There's been talk of putting an art gallery on the first floor."

"Art's not my strong suit, miss, but while they're building it, the construction noise is going to disturb me and everyone else for at least the next eight months."

Suddenly, a loud bang on the wood boards of the sidewalk behind Nora startled her. Turning around, she saw the movers attempting to get a grip on a large oak desk that had slipped out of their hands.

"I should arrest you two for defacing city property!" Englund yelled.

"I hope you find those file boxes," Nora said, as she hurried away.

When she arrived at the corner of Ocean and Dolores, she paused to inspect a nearly-completed building that could have been the Forest Theater's backdrop for one of Herbert Heron's Shakespearean plays. With its white stucco walls decorated with intermittent half-timbers, the structure resembled an English Tudor-style cottage. She had never seen a roof like this one. All the edges were tightly rolled wood shingles that formed a distinctive curved overhang.

Nora recognized the young woman who was walking about inside the empty building. Ruth Kuster had a reputation in town as an expert weaver who exhibited her handiwork in many of the village shops. Slender, attractive, with a short dark bob, the wife of Carmel's theater entrepreneur, Edward Kuster, waved at her and stepped outside.

"Hello, Nora," she said in a cheerful voice. "How do you like my new studio? I'm working hard to open the shop in September. I hope you'll come visit me then, and I promise to give you a weaving lesson, along with a tour of the place."

"I'd like that. Good luck, Ruth, and please give my regards to your husband."

Nora continued on to the *Pine Cone*'s office in the next block. When she opened the front door, she was instantly greeted with enthusiasm by Mary Lee Owens.

"I missed you terribly, Nora," the short, plump, sandy-haired woman said. Getting up from her desk and coming around the reception counter, the publisher's wife stood on tiptoes to give her a hug.

"I missed you too," Nora replied, as she kissed the older woman on the cheek. "I know your train arrived late, and you probably didn't sleep well last night, but I'm so glad you came into the office today. It hasn't been the same around here without you. I know it must have been very hard to leave your mother."

Mary Lee's eyes filled with tears. "That's true. She and my father were very close. But I have my family here in Carmel to take care of. That includes you. Tell me what's been going on since Sally and I left for Chicago."

For the next few minutes, Nora provided the *Pine Cone*'s receptionist with every detail surrounding Guy Porter's murder and the progress in the sheriff's investigation. She didn't mention last night's visit to Egan's roadhouse in Carmel Valley. The less said about it the better.

Grateful that the telephone hadn't interrupted their conversation, Nora said, "I've been so eager to ask you what you know about the playwright, James Carpenter. His play has been cancelled because of all the bad publicity."

"Well, I knew his former wife, but that was a long time ago. When they were divorced, she returned to San Francisco where she had grown up and James remained here in Carmel, where he joined the Western Drama Society's board of directors. Since then, he's immersed himself in local theater. He's quite well-off financially, and he has remained a bachelor married to his profession."

Nora thought of Vera Winfield. "He may not be a bachelor much longer."

"Really? Is there a new woman in James' life since I've

been gone?"

The telephone rang.

"I guess I'll have to wait a little longer to hear the latest gossip," Mary Lee said.

Nora went to her desk and sat down. She removed her typewriter cover, and for the rest of the morning, concentrated on the weekly assignments Mr. Owens gave her to write about before each Wednesday's issue. In between writing her articles, her thoughts drifted to Sheriff Jimmy Connery. He was an experienced investigator who might be able to locate the cowboy who had assaulted Vera last night. Nora fretted over how Jimmy would react when he discovered that she had gone to Egan's roadhouse with the Preston brothers.

She didn't have very long to wait.

The wall clock struck noon as the front door opened and the tall figure of Monterey County's top lawman strolled in. "Are you free for lunch, Nora?" he asked, as he came up to her desk. "I hope so, because I have a few things to discuss with you. How about joining me at the Blue Bird Tea Room?"

"All right. They usually have one or two free tables during the week days."

Nora reached for her purse and stood up. She was surprised that Jimmy had suggested the one place where they had enjoyed spending time together during the past six months.

Holding the door for her, he mumbled, "Keep in mind, this is business, and not a social call."

"That's perfectly fine with me."

Although they walked side-by-side to the nearby tearoom, Jimmy didn't take her arm to guide her across Dolores Street. After being shown to a table for two and menus provided to them, they both ordered ham sandwiches and a pot of Darjeeling tea.

Jimmy spoke first. "I brought a copy of the county coroner's official autopsy report regarding Guy Porter. His sister claimed his body and is taking it to San Francisco for burial."

"I feel very sorry for her loss. Was the coroner's conclusion the same as that of Doctor Barnes?"

Handing Nora an official-looking document, Jimmy continued, "The coroner found that Porter's mouth and throat sustained a caustic burn reaction from his swallowing muriatic acid. His upper airway and pharynx were swollen shut. When someone pulled out his breathing tube, he died of suffocation."

"It sounds like a horrible death. Whoever did this to Guy must have had a powerful motive."

Just then, the waitress reappeared with their food.

Jimmy bit into his sandwich and said, "I spoke with the French girl, Renee Lucien, and took her statement. She said that she and Victor Wolfe spent the night together when Porter died. That gives him an airtight alibi. Wolfe is not the murderer."

"Do you plan to hold him on assault charges for his part in trying to harm Guy?"

"Of course. It's attempted assault. Wolfe denies bribing the stagehand to loosen the backdrop so it would fall on Porter and injure him. I've talked to Tommy Anderson and got a statement from him." Taking a sip of tea, Jimmy put down his cup and looked directly at Nora. "When were you going to tell me you visited that speakeasy in Carmel Valley last night?"

Nora felt her face and neck getting red. "Look, I didn't know I was being taken there. I was simply going out for a driving lesson, that's all."

"That's a flimsy excuse. This is a serious matter, Nora. I'm not saying Egan is corrupt, but his bar in the back is illegal and some of his patrons are lowlifes. Those kinds of places are dangerous, especially for an unattached young woman like you. You should have asked to be brought back home."

Nora put down her sandwich. She had lost her appetite. "Stop moralizing about my behavior and tell me if you've located the cowboy who tried to kill Vera Winfield."

Jimmy shook his head. "Egan thinks someone hired him to attack Miss Winfield. He told the marshal and me that he had never seen the man in his place before."

"What I can't understand is why he made a bee-line for Vera as soon as we appeared."

"There's an explanation for that. Egan's waitress said she saw the cowboy staring at all the young women who came in last night. But he went right over to Vera as soon as the three of you sat down."

Nora shuddered. "So someone deliberately stalked her with the intent to kill her. Are you going to talk to her? If you are, I can be of help to you. She trusts me because I found her in the shed as the attack was occurring. She believes that I saved her life."

"You probably did, and I'm going over to the San Carlos Lodge to interview her when we're finished eating. However, this is strictly police business. I don't need you."

Getting up, Nora said, "I'm sorry you feel that way, Sheriff. Shall we go?"

Jimmy paid the bill and escorted her back to the newspaper office. While he stood at the publisher's door and conversed with Mr. Owens, the telephone rang.

"Nora," Mary Lee piped up, "it's Mrs. Stevens on the line."

Going to her desk, Nora picked up and listened to the woman's brief message. Before putting down the receiver, she said, "Thanks for letting me know, Annie."

Hearing her mention Annie's name, Jimmy looked over at her. "What did Vera Winfield's landlady have to say?"

"Even though you expressly said you don't need me to be involved in police business, I'll tell you what I know and you don't."

Jimmy frowned. "All right then. Tell me."

"There's no need for you to head over to the San Carlos Lodge."

"And why is that?"

"Because Annie called me to say that Vera has disappeared."

CHAPTER TWENTY THREE

Nora trailed behind Jimmy to his black sheriff's sedan parked a block away from the newspaper office. She was not going to be deterred by his abrupt attitude. She said, "Sheriff, I want you to tell me something. Did you check Victor Wolfe's fingerprints with the ones that were on the pint bottle of milk somebody threw in the bushes next to the stage?"

Opening the driver's side door, he said, "Yes, and they're not Wolfe's. Since you're bound to find out anyway, I'll also tell you this. After we determined Wolfe was not the murderer, Marshal Englund and I talked to Burt Erickson again. He still couldn't remember anything or provide a shred of useful information about what went on back stage at the Forest Theater at the time Guy Porter was poisoned."

"I wouldn't expect him to. He was unconscious."

"You just don't understand police investigative techniques, Miss Reporter. All we had was his word. Repeating a story sometimes brings out inconsistencies or even forgotten remembrances. It was Erickson's job to set up your tea tray. He continues to claim that he didn't touch it that night. He said that somebody hit him on the head, filled the cream pitcher, added the muriatic acid, and brought the tray to the table where you found it. But I still have the distinct impression that he's holding something back."

"Then why don't you take Burt's fingerprints so you can rule him out? For that matter, what about Tommy the stagehand? You know that he took a bribe from Victor. Someone might have paid him to doctor the cream pitcher with acid."

He grinned for the first time. "I should make you my deputy. I already did that, Nora. Neither man's fingerprints match those on the milk bottle."

"I'm convinced that the person who poisoned Guy Porter is somehow linked to the Forest Theater. How else could he have known our rehearsal routine?"

"Well, if you have any other worthwhile suggestions, I'll be happy to consider them. Otherwise, I don't want you interfering in any way with this investigation. I'd better be going."

"You haven't gotten over being irked at me, have you? You've done nothing but demean and criticize me now, as well as during lunch."

He put his hand on her forearm. "I'll tell you why I'm irked. You went to Egan's roadhouse, a place of ill repute, and you chased after Vera Winfield's attacker. You could have been hurt. I won't have someone who might be Molly's future stepmother acting so foolishly."

Pushing his hand away, Nora said, "You are so judgmental, Jimmy Connery. It's a good thing that we're no longer a couple!" She turned to go before she said something more that she would later regret.

"Come back here!" he shouted.

Nora had never heard him speak so harshly. "You can forget about my having dinner with you tonight," she said in a low voice, as she walked away.

·

"What's wrong, Nora?" Mary Lee said when she returned to the office. "I can tell by your face that you're upset. Did something happen between you and Jimmy?"

"If you don't mind, Mary Lee, I'd rather not discuss the sheriff's poor attitude." Going to the closet, Nora hung up the pressed skirt that she had picked up at Ki Mee's Laundry and returned to stand in front of the receptionist's desk. "I'm sorry," she said, "but I'm in no mood to explain how I feel."

"All right, but if you do want to tell me about it, I'm here and ready to listen. By the way, there were two telephone messages for you while you were gone. Mrs. Stevens called again, and she sounded upset."

"Who was the other caller?"

"Burt Erickson. He wondered if you had time to stop by his place this afternoon. He said he'd be there until four. Then he would be at the theater doing some chores for the rest of the evening."

"I don't think I can settle down and work on any story right now. I would like to go over to see Annie at the lodge, and find out what she's worried about. A brisk walk will do me good. Then I'll stop by Burt's place. If Mr. Owens asks about me, tell him I should be back in about an hour."

"Don't worry. I'll take care of it."

Nora felt the afternoon breeze coming up from the beach as she shut the office door. Pausing to stare across Ocean Avenue, she thought she recognized the tall young man making his way through the row of young bushy pines the city had planted to create the main street's median. His black suit and leather bag identified him even before he was close enough for her to actually see his face.

Zachary Barnes, Carmel's new physician, smiled and tipped his hat. "I thought that was you, Miss Finnegan. Where are you heading on this beautiful day?"

His friendliness instantly brought Nora out of her foul mood. Smiling back, she said, "I'm working on a story for the newspaper, but I wish I could play hooky instead. It would be a perfect time to go beachcombing down by the cove, don't you think?"

"I'm guessing that's why the first Bohemians came to live in Carmel. You know what? Let's do just that some weekend. I could use a little relaxation."

Nora nodded. "Being employed fulltime has its obstacles, but my job isn't as demanding as yours is. You're on call day and night. We should get together at your convenience."

"Sometime soon I hope to persuade another doctor to settle here and share some of my responsibilities. But we don't have to wait until then. Let's plan something around our busy schedules for this Sunday. We can get better acquainted."

Her sometime relationship with Jimmy had just terminated, and her interest in Lee Preston revolved around driving lessons. She said, "I'd like that."

"Good. How about meeting me at two o'clock in front of the Bath House? We can hike out to Pescadero Point. I don't know what the weather will be like, but if you believe the prediction I see each day on the blackboard at Leidig's grocery store, it should be overcast around this time of the day."

Nora laughed. "I'll do what all Carmelites do here in the summertime — wear an extra layer of clothing. I'd better be going. I'll see you this Sunday at two."

The doctor tipped his hat and went into Staniford's Drug Store. Nora picked up her pace to Annie Stevens' boarding house a few blocks away. She could feel her spirits lifting with each step.

"Thank goodness, it's you," Annie said. Giving her a hug, she ushered Nora into the front room. "I've been on pins and needles, ever since the sheriff left a few minutes ago. I told him what I told you on the telephone. Vera's gone and I have no idea where she went. She left early this morning before I got up. I'm so worried about her, Nora. Would you ask around and see if you can locate her?"

"I know she was frightened, but I never thought she would leave without telling anyone — especially you, Annie. Perhaps Mr. Carpenter came back and she's gone off with him. Does she have any close relatives nearby?"

"She grew up in Southern California. She told me her ma died a couple years ago and Vera wasn't all that close to her dad."

"Let's see how many clothes she took with her. Would it be all right if I take a look around her bedroom? There might be something that would give us a clue as to where she went."

"What a good idea, Nora. Go right on up. I'll be in the kitchen."

Nora stepped into Vera's room. The bed had been left unmade and the closet door was ajar. She saw a few empty hangers inside and a couple of vacant spaces on the floor where Vera's shoes had been lined up. The actress was traveling light. Stepping over to the dresser, she glanced at the wide open drawers. It looked as if only a few pieces of lingerie had been removed, as well as a sweater. Vera had gone into temporary hiding somewhere close by. More than likely, she was with James Carpenter.

Pulling up the bedcovers, Nora noticed a notebook lying among its folds. Thumbing through it, she saw it was a journal. When she put it down, a loose picture fell out onto the pillowcase. She stared down at a small photograph of Vera in a revealing bathing costume, her shoulder length red hair looking more natural than the marcelled waves the actress currently favored.

But what held her attention were the two young men who were standing on each side of Vera. Wearing two-piece, wool tank tops and belted swim trunks, the taller one, Lee Preston, had his left hand on her bare shoulder. The other man was a bit stockier, but Nora easily recognized the face of Tex, the cowboy from Egan's roadhouse. She turned the photograph over. On the back was a handwritten note: Having fun on the set of "Foolish Wives," near Carmel-By-The-Sea, California, 1920. *That confirms that Vera had known Lee in Hollywood before his trip to the Bohemian Club in San Francisco last April. She also knew Tex.* Inserting the picture between two pages, she left the notebook on the bed.

As she was about to leave, she stopped in front of the dresser. Vera's hairbrush was gone. So was the crystal bottle of "Chanel." However, a residue of the perfume remained in the spot where the vial had formerly stood. Nora slid her index finger across it and dabbed a tiny bit of the spicy fragrance behind her ear. Then she went to find Annie downstairs.

CHAPTER TWENTY FOUR

Nora left the lodge and headed down San Carlos Street to Tenth. She passed the shuttered Sunset School that would remain that way until September, when Carmel's young students returned. At the corner of Mission Street, she turned right and almost tripped over Burt Erickson's Labrador lying on the dirt path leading up to his cabin. The dog didn't get up or bark at her. Blackie was too busy gnawing on a tattered canvas shoe.

"Some watchdog I have there," Burt called out, as he stepped off his front porch and walked down the steps to meet her.

Nora noticed that he hadn't shaved for days and his head remained bandaged. She said, "Hi, Burt. How are you feeling today?"

"I'm glad you came by," he said. "I'm doing pretty good, but I had to call you, miss. Something's been bothering me and... ." Without warning, he suddenly jumped backwards. His foot landed on one of Blackie's paws. The Labrador leaped up, dropped his toy and whined loudly as he limped away.

"Oh, my gosh. I didn't mean to do that," Burt said. He went over and knelt down next to the dog to comfort him. While petting him, he avoided looking up at Nora.

"What's the matter?" she said. "Does your head wound make you dizzy?"

Getting to his feet, Burt cast a sidelong glance at her. "It's not me I'm fretting over. Do you mind if I get closer to you? I promise I won't hurt you."

Nora wasn't sure what he meant by that, but she said, "All right, come ahead."

Standing beside her, he pushed back some of her hair and sniffed her neck. Then he stepped back, a puzzled look on his face. "That toilet water of yours," he mumbled, "where'd you get it?"

"It's perfume, Burt. I sort of borrowed it. Why do you want to know?"

Scratching at his bandage, the prop man didn't answer. He climbed up on the porch and took a seat on the top step. "Come sit by me."

"Won't you tell me what's wrong?" she said, as she sat down next to him.

"I don't know exactly. I asked you to come over here to see me because I remembered an odd thing after I got my wits back from being attacked the other day. I thought about telling the sheriff when he came by, but I knew he'd laugh at me."

"You can tell me. I wouldn't make fun of you."

He sighed. "Well, just before I got socked on the back of my head, I got a whiff of that same stuff you've got on, miss. Now I am confused. Could it have been a lady that hit me? Was it you?"

Vera's perfume! "You remembering that smell could be a very important clue, Burt. It points to your attacker and maybe whoever poisoned Guy Porter. But it definitely wasn't me. Are you sure you weren't imagining the smell?"

"I don't know for sure. That's my problem. If you think it's important though, you tell the sheriff. I don't want to be kidded for being an old fool who dreams about young ladies."

"Don't be silly. I'll follow up on it for you. And I think you should cancel going to the theater today. Stay home for another day or two."

"I need to work. Who else will pay my rent and buy food for Blackie?"

Hearing his name called, the Labrador cocked his head and wagged his tail. Apparently, he had recovered and was ready to forgive his master's clumsiness. Stretched out at the foot of the steps, the dog began chewing again on his favorite shoe.

Nora strode into Levy's like a woman on a mission. She savored the warmth of afternoon sun streaming through the general store's large plate glass windows, while a thumping overhead fan fluffed the top of her hair and moved the store's stale air out.

Joseph Levy stood behind a display counter, pulling out several varieties of fishing lures and waiting on a customer. Seeing her enter, the proprietor called out, "Afternoon, Miss Finnegan. Take a look around while I finish up here."

"Hello, Mr. Levy. It's a delightful day, isn't it?"

"Can't do nothing about it, even if I wanted to."

Nora laughed.

Turning around, Levy's customer smiled and tipped his hat. It was Randall King.

"Hello, Nora. How are you?" he said. "I miss our play rehearsals. It's too bad they've been put off indefinitely."

"I miss them too, Randall."

"Have you heard anything more about James Carpenter's restraining order? I was wondering if a judge has been assigned to hear it. I'm sure both James and Lee Preston are anxious to get this behind them, so at least one of their plays can go forward."

"I'm sorry, but I haven't any news on that score. I've noticed that it takes the court about two or three weeks to schedule hearings."

Randall shook his head. "That miserable Carpenter still hasn't paid me for the rehearsals. Now he has another excuse for delay. Unless my chauffeuring job picks up, I'm going to have more free time on my hands and less money in my pocket. That's why I'm here, Nora. Tommy, our stagehand, is out of a job too. He invited me to go fishing with him on the Carmel River this Saturday."

"I hope the fish are biting. My father would envy you two. River fishing is his favorite pastime." Looking over at Joseph Levy, Nora added, "Oh, I nearly forgot. I came in to see your perfume selection."

"What I have in stock is located in the ladies ready-to-wear section, Miss Finnegan. I'll come join you, as soon as I've helped Mr. King with his purchase."

Nora found the glass display case nestled among rows of hanging dresses, skirts and petticoats. The various bottles of all shapes and sizes were nothing like the elaborately decorated Baccarat and Lalique crystal perfume bottles on her mother's bedroom dresser. Levy's selections were plainer looking, and she saw nothing like the "Chanel" bottle with its delicate, rounded shoulders.

"Now how may I help you, Miss Finnegan?" Levy said, as he walked up.

His ample girth, white beard, pink cheeks and round spectacles would always remind her of Santa Claus, a role he played during the holidays. From her very first visit to Carmel, when she sat on his lap and told him her secrets, he had amused her no end every Christmas. "I'm looking for a fragrance called 'Chanel.' It's named after Coco Chanel, the French clothing designer."

"I've read about her in the Monterey newspaper. My wife prefers toilet water, not one of those fancy French colognes. By the way, is that 'Chanel' you're wearing, Miss Finnegan? It's pretty alluring."

Nora saw his face turn red.

"Forgive my lack of manners. I shouldn't be asking a young lady such a personal question."

She smiled at him. "You haven't offended me, Mr. Levy. If you don't carry the 'Chanel' brand, I wonder if you might know where I can find it."

"There's no market for it around here. We're still Bohemians and worldly in lots of ways, but when it comes to spending money for extravagant things, I'm afraid we prefer the simpler life. But I think I can help you. Why don't I telephone the City of Paris department store in San Francisco and ask if they carry that brand of perfume?"

"That would be wonderful." Nora remembered that Vera's hat boxes had come from the City of Paris. "And while I wait for the information, I'll browse through your selection of summer clothes."

"Be right back then."

When he returned to the ladies wear section, Levy said, "I have disappointing news, Miss Finnegan. It isn't possible to buy 'Chanel' perfume anywhere." Seeing her look of surprise, he continued, "I couldn't believe it either, but that's what the woman told me. Although Miss Chanel has been producing her perfume in France for the past three years, she gives it only as gifts to select customers in her Paris boutique. The saleslady claimed that the little glass bottles were too delicate to ship and distribute to American customers. It seems that one must travel to Paris to obtain it."

Hiding her disappointment, Nora said, "Thank you for finding out about it."

"No trouble." Pointing at the clothes rack behind her, he said, "By the way, I'll tell you a secret. Don't buy anything now. My ladies summer wear will be going on sale the first week of August."

"Thanks. I'll be sure to remember that," Nora said, as she

waved goodbye.

On her way back to the *Pine Cone* office, she heard a man's voice calling to her from across Ocean Avenue. Turning around, she saw Keith shutting and locking the library's front door. How odd, she thought. It was far too early to close the place on a Thursday afternoon.

He ran across the street and joined her on the sidewalk. "Have you seen or talked to Lee today? I'm getting concerned about him."

"No, I haven't, Keith. Why are you so worried?"

"Ever since the judge suspended his play, Lee's been in a horrible state of mind. He's moody and irritable. I tried calling him at the Pine Inn this morning, but he wasn't in his room. He usually stops by the library at lunchtime, but he didn't come in today. I've been waiting and waiting to hear from him. I finally decided to go over to the hotel and see what he was up to. The bell boy said he saw him leave the hotel very early this morning and he hasn't returned."

"I'm sure he's perfectly fine. More than likely, he's taking advantage of this warm weather and gone for a ride along the coast." *Could Lee have taken Vera with him to keep her safe from further attacks?* Leaning over, Nora gave her friend a quick hug.

"Where did you get that perfume you're wearing?" Keith asked.

When she didn't answer immediately, he said, "You see, my mother told me it's only available to Coco Chanel's special clients. Mother gets it in Paris while she's clothes shopping each season. She always brings a few bottles home with her to give as gifts. I'll bet Lee gave you a vial, didn't he?"

Nora gasped. She had just learned a secret that no one else knew.

CHAPTER TWENTY FIVE

Friday

With half the bedclothes on the floor, it was evident to Nora that she hadn't slept much during the night. Shutting off the alarm clock at six o'clock, she got out of bed, found her bathrobe, and stumbled into the kitchen. While she waited for the teapot's water to boil, she continued mulling over Vera's unexplained disappearance, Keith's story about his mother's French perfume, and even her heated argument with Jimmy. As she was buttering a slice of toast, she heard the telephone ring in the front room.

"Did I wake you?" Keith's excited voice jarred her ears. "No one's seen Lee since yesterday, Nora, and he hasn't called me. I asked the manager at the Pine Inn to check his room. Not only hasn't it been slept in, but his automobile's gone."

"He's a grown man, Keith. Isn't he entitled to some privacy? I'm sure there's a logical explanation as to why he hasn't been in touch."

"I don't agree. I'm about to call the marshal and ask him to start looking. I think he's being blackmailed. Why else would he want all that money from our trust fund? Now it makes sense to me. My brother's afraid of someone and he's gone into hiding."

"Stop that! You're overreacting, in my opinion. Let me relieve your anxiety by checking around the village this morning."

"Would you do that? It would ease my mind. I have an important library meeting in Monterey all day today and it's impossible for me to get out of it."

"Someone has probably seen Lee at the Forest Theater or in one of the shops," Nora said. "Now calm down and focus on your work. I'll telephone you at home this evening. By then, one of us will have heard from him."

Hanging up the receiver, Nora wasn't so sure. Maybe she should have confided her suspicions to Keith that his brother and Vera might be together. She didn't believe it was a coincidence that both of them were missing — especially upon finding out that they had known one another for several years.

After cleaning up the breakfast dishes, she hurried to her room to get dressed. She had to be at the office on time today, to put together a pair of stories that Mr. Owens had expressly requested she write for the *Pine Cone*'s upcoming issue. Luckily, Mary Lee would be helping out by responding to all the newspaper's telephone callers.

By eight o'clock, Nora was sitting behind her typewriter. She worked for two hours on her article about Edward Kuster's proposed playhouse on Ocean Avenue, but she had difficulty focusing on the other one concerning the recent opening of Grimshaw's Flying A gasoline station at the corner of San Carlos and Sixth Avenue. No matter how hard she tried, she couldn't stop thinking about yesterday's events.

She didn't know exactly what to make of Burt's smelling the distinctive "Chanel" perfume before someone attacked him. That, together with Keith's remark that his mother had brought the same perfume home with her from Paris, directly implicated Vera, and more than likely Lee, in Burt's assault. Also, her discovery of their photograph taken at a place near Carmel where a movie was being filmed, confirmed their prior relationship, as well as both knowing the man who had attacked Vera at Egan's.

Her thoughts were interrupted by the publisher coming out of his office. "Are you finished with those stories?" he asked, as he stopped in front of her desk. "I want to typeset them before I go to lunch."

Nora pulled the filling station article out of her typewriter and picked up the finished one about the new theater. Handing both to him, she said, "I know you're busy, Mr. Owens, but would you spare me a few minutes? I have so much information swirling in my head about the Porter murder story that I need someone to hear it and help clarify some confusing points."

Mary Lee had been listening to them. "I'll make sure that no one interrupts either of you with a telephone call," she said.

Owens nodded at his wife and led the way to his office.

Nora pulled up a chair and sat down as he settled behind his desk.

"I'm very interested in what you think about the case, Honora."

She began by sharing Burt's account of the "Chanel" perfume and mentioned where she thought it had come from. "But what I'm having trouble believing is that Vera, perhaps with the help of Keith's brother, was responsible for Guy Porter's death."

Owens rubbed his chin. "How would either of them get hold of the acid?"

"That's what makes it more plausible. You know Ben Turner, the brick mason?"

"Yes, he's a good man. He fixed a faulty fireplace for me last winter. How does he fit into the picture?"

"He's in the process of building a new wall at the San Carlos Lodge for Annie Stevens. He's using muriatic acid to clean kelp off abalone shells that will decorate the wall. He showed me a container full of acid in the lodge's back yard. Vera, who lives there, could have found out about it."

"Well, that would certainly give her access to it."

"I agree. She could easily have taken some of it when Turner wasn't there. The sheriff has yet to identify whose fingerprints are on the milk bottle that was used in Porter's poisoning, but I'm guessing they could be Vera's."

Owens looked puzzled. "But what motive could she have for injuring Porter?"

Nora shrugged. "I think she helped Lee create havoc at the Forest Theater by putting acid into a cream pitcher, and Lee did other things to keep Carpenter's play from being performed. His story about Victor Wolfe, Porter's understudy, convinced the sheriff to arrest him. Lee then persuaded the theater board to cancel Carpenter's play."

Owens sat back in his chair. "So you're saying that they plotted to remove both lead actors so the Forest Theater Society's board would vote to pick Lee's play."

"Yes, but they've had a bit of a setback. Carpenter announced that he would assume the leading man's role, and last night he went to the lodge to tell Vera that he was giving her Claudia Jacklin's part. I know how much Vera covets it. I think she posed a dilemma for Lee, and he has taken her somewhere to keep Vera from being in the play."

"You're becoming a good investigative reporter, Honora. Your father would be very proud of you."

Nora stood up to go. "Thank you for giving me this job, Mr. Owens. I know I was inexperienced to start with, and as a friend of my father, you did him a favor by hiring me."

Coming around the desk, he put his hands on her shoulders. "Having known you since childhood, I want to give you some fatherly advice. Mrs. Owens says you're having difficulty communicating with Sheriff Connery. You need to get past whatever has transpired between you two. Reporters have to deal with emotional events. They can't be swayed by them."

Dropping his hands, he stepped away. "Contact the sheriff as soon as possible. Tell Jimmy what you've told me. What you found out is critical to his investigation."

Nora knew he was right. "I'll telephone him now," she said.

They heard a soft rap on the door. Mary Lee peeked in. "I'm sorry to disturb you, William, but Marshal Englund is on the telephone. He told me there was a break-in at the drug store — something connected to the Porter murder."

"I'll take his call. Stay right there, Honora. This could be important."

A few moments later, Owens put down the receiver and looked over at her. "Marshal Englund said that several glass beakers that Doc had stored in the back room were smashed to pieces last night. One of them was the beaker with the milk sample containing the muriatic acid."

CHAPTER TWENTY SIX

Following Mr. Owens' advice, Nora returned to her desk and placed a telephone call to the county sheriff's office in Monterey.

"It's good to hear from you, Miss Finnegan," Senior Deputy Alvin Jensen said, when he picked up. "If you're calling about talking to that actor, Victor Wolfe, I'm afraid you're too late. I drove him to the main jail in Salinas last night. His attorney can't convince him to plead guilty to attempted assault. Wolfe claims he was only trying to scare the other actor into going back to San Francisco, so he could take his place."

"I'm not trying to interview Mr. Wolfe, Deputy Jensen. I want to speak to your boss. Is Sheriff Connery available?"

"Your luck's holding today, miss. He's right here. I'll put you through."

As she waited, Nora felt unsettled. She didn't relish confronting Jimmy again after their unfriendly parting yesterday. When he came on the line, she said, "I don't want you to interrupt me for any reason until I finish what I have to say." She then told him in detail what she had told Mr. Owens a few minutes ago.

He didn't reply for what seemed to Nora much too long a time. "Are you there?" she asked.

He answered with a grunt. Finally, in a tone that sounded dismissive, he said, "That's all conjecture. You don't have anything that I would call evidence to back up what you're saying, Miss Finnegan. You talked to some old guy who thinks he smelled a whiff of French cologne before he got hit on the head. Did he also tell you that he had a vision of the pearly gates?"

He was throwing out some bait to start an argument. I'm not biting.

When she didn't say anything, Jimmy continued, "You found an old picture of the person who assaulted Miss Winfield. You did that by rummaging around someone's private room without permission. And you assume the muriatic acid that was put in the cream pitcher used in your play came from a bucket in Mrs. Stevens' back yard."

"Quit making light of what I'm telling you. I know I don't have the evidence. I thought it was your job to gather it."

"That's exactly my point. What you're doing is making my investigation more difficult. If I remember my last words to you, I asked you to keep out of police business."

Nora was furious. "No, those weren't your last words, Sheriff. As I recall, they were: 'Come back here!'"

After a loud sigh, he said, "O.K. Nora. I hear what you're telling me, and I appreciate the information, but it's not the kind of solid evidence I need. Moreover, you could taint it by probing around."

"Do you or don't you want to take a look at the photograph I found? It proves that Vera Winfield was acquainted with Lee Preston years ago, as well as identifying the man who attacked her at Egan's."

"As you know, if I want to see that picture, and use it as evidence, I'll need a search warrant. There are laws about that."

When Nora didn't answer, he said, "Let me do this. If Miss Winfield is truly missing because someone has taken her somewhere without her consent, and her landlady substantiates that, I'll get an order to search her room and pick up the photograph you saw. I'll also talk to Burt Erickson to confirm what he told you."

For once he was being cooperative. "Call Annie Stevens as soon as we're finished talking, Jimmy."

"Don't tell me how to do my job."

Nora bit her lip and hung up.

After numerous long distance telephone calls, and a few dead ends, Nora finally got a good lead. A Hollywood studio publicist named Dan White listened to her story and agreed to research the location where "Foolish Wives" had been filmed.

Half an hour later, White returned Nora's call. "Here's what you're looking for, Miss Finnegan. The film's production crew scouted the central coast and selected a place called Point Lobos. According to their publicity, they built an enormous outdoor set resembling a Mediterranean villa there. In one of the still photographs, Japanese divers are seen harvesting abalone on the rocks below the villa. The newspaper article I have in my file reported that the divers shared their daily catch with the cast and crew."

"What else did you find out about the making of the movie, Mr. White? I'd like my story to hold our newspaper readers' interest."

"O. K., wait another minute then." Shuffling some papers, White came back on the line. "Here's a fact you can use. The studio claimed this was the first movie to cost a million dollars to make. They put up an electronic sign on a New York City rooftop overlooking Broadway that kept people entertained as to the final production costs. They updated it weekly, but some said it only came to $700,000 dollars."

"That's amazing. You've been very helpful, Mr. White, and if it isn't too much trouble, I'm trying to get information on a screenwriter who's worked in Hollywood for several years. Perhaps you know him? His name is Lee Preston."

There was a moment of silence. "I'd be careful if I were you," White finally said. "I heard Preston's branched out into much bigger things. Here's what I know."

His information shocked Nora, but it explained Lee's recent appearance before Carmel's Planning Commission. She thanked the publicist for his help and hung up.

Pulling off her typewriter cover, she remembered something that Ben Turner, the local brick mason, had said. Annie Stevens found the abalone shells he was using on the wall he was building for her at Whalers Cove. It must be close to the "Foolish Wives" movie set, given the presence of Japanese abalone divers in that area. There could also be some private accommodations nearby where people coming from out of the area could stay. Could Vera have gone there, she wondered?

During her lunch hour, Nora walked around the village and up the hill to the Forest Theater to ask if anyone had seen or spoken to Lee Preston. No one had. Returning to the office, she started on two new assignments that Mr. Owens had left on her desk. While she worked them up, she couldn't stop thinking about Vera and Lee.

Despite the sheriff's warning, by four o'clock, Nora made a decision to act on what she thought was a logical conclusion. Picking up the telephone, she gave the operator a local number.

James Carpenter said, "Hello."

"It's Nora Finnegan, James. I'm at the *Pine Cone* office. Did you know that Vera left the lodge early yesterday morning without telling anyone where she was going?"

"I called there this morning and asked to speak to her. Annie said that she didn't know where Vera was. I've been sitting here, half out of my wits with worry."

"I have an idea where she might be. It involves a drive and it could be a wild goose chase. Would you be interested in taking a chance that I could be right?"

"Absolutely. I can meet you in ten minutes at the corner of San Carlos and Ocean," the director said. "I'll be driving a blue Buick sedan with a black soft top."

"I'll be waiting there for you," Nora said, as she opened her desk's bottom drawer and reached for her purse. Getting up, she looked over at Mary Lee. "I'm leaving early today. James Carpenter and I are driving out to Whalers Cove."

The receptionist winked. "Isn't he a bit old for you, Nora?"

CHAPTER TWENTY SEVEN

Before they left the village, James made a stop at Grimshaw's Flying A. Nora had just finished writing her story about the place and recognized the attendant who stepped out of the new Mission-styled filling station to approach the sedan.

Tapping his thumb on the steering wheel, James looked annoyed. "Larry," he said, "eighteen cents a gallon is awfully steep. The stations in Monterey charge a lot less than that for their gasoline."

"It's a low price, sir, when you consider we have to ship it over the Carmel hill," the young man replied. "So do you want some gas or don't you, Mr. Carpenter?"

James frowned and handed him a couple of dollars. "Fill the tank."

From her vantage point in the front passenger seat, Nora was surprised by how much Larry did after he put gasoline in the tank. He washed the windshield, checked the air in the tires, and even lifted the hood to top off the radiator. She had never realized that owning an automobile took so much maintenance. Still, she was determined to buy a two-seater roadster as soon as she learned to drive.

When they were ready to leave, Nora watched carefully

as James pushed the clutch pedal with his left foot, engaged the Buick's low gear, released the hand-brake and applied his foot to the gas pedal. The car moved smoothly forward. At the top of Ocean Avenue, he stopped and checked for oncoming traffic from the north. Seeing none, he pulled out onto the two lane county road. Nora welcomed the impromptu driving lesson.

They headed south towards Big Sur. Paying strict attention to everything James did, she saw him apply the foot brake several times to slow their descent as they approached the wooden plank bridge over the Carmel River. Although it was nearly five o'clock, a clear sky and bright sun kept the air streaming through the car's open cabin warm and pleasant. As they bumped across the bridge, she could hear the ocean's waves impacting the river's downstream run. She thought it must be high tide.

Not knowing whether they would even find the actress, Nora decided to be candid with James. "You probably wonder how I came to the conclusion that Vera might be out at Whalers Cove."

"Did her landlady suggest it to her?"

"Yes, Annie said if Vera was afraid of being attacked again, she had friends out there who would take her in."

"If she was so frightened, why didn't Vera come to me? Heaven's knows, I have plenty of room at my place. I live alone."

"That could cause a lot of local gossip, which I'm sure Vera wouldn't relish."

"I'll let you in on a secret, Nora. I'm in love with Vera and I'm going to ask her to be my wife as soon as we find her. I only hope that she accepts my proposal."

Hiding her astonishment, Nora turned away to watch a Model T pickup truck that was slowing down on a side road. She noticed that the flatbed was stacked with tied-down crates of leafy vegetables. Rather than come to a full stop before turning, the driver suddenly pulled out in front of them. "He's not a cautious driver like you are," she said.

James shrugged but didn't respond. Instead, he drove up close to the truck's rear, downshifted to another gear, then braked suddenly. Nora could tell that he was provoked. Finally, the truck driver slowed down to a crawl. James craned his head out his window and saw no one was traveling towards them. Honking his horn in frustration, he pulled out into the oncoming lane and accelerated.

As they passed, Nora looked over at the truck driver, who couldn't have been more than sixteen. Wearing a floppy straw hat and coveralls, the boy was steering the truck with one hand and waved at her with the other. She smiled. He might be learning to drive too.

Rows of gnarled cypress trees bordered the road up ahead. They traveled at a steady pace and met no other vehicles. Settling back in his seat, James said, "Years ago, there used to be a narrow-gauge railroad running out here."

"Was it for the tourists who wanted to visit Point Lobos?" Nora asked.

He chuckled. "No, it was used to haul sand out to the ships anchored in Whalers Cove. It was strictly a commercial endeavor. I first learned about the railroad's presence half a dozen years ago when I drove out to Point Lobos to watch some of the filming of 'The Valley of the Moon.' From that time on, all I wanted to do was direct movies. In the end, I had to settle for plays, because I preferred living here and not in Southern California."

His comment caused Nora to ask, "Did you see 'Foolish Wives' when it was filmed at Whalers Cove?"

"No, I would have liked to, but I was involved in a messy divorce and all my attention was focused on that." Both of them caught sight of the "Point Lobos" sign at the same time.

"It looks like we're here," Nora said.

James turned onto a bumpy, dusty road and headed toward the ocean.

The sun was beginning to set, but the day was still bright. Driving through an open gate, they entered a dense grove of Monterey pines. Beneath them, Nora spotted stands of evergreen shrubs, including the colorful lizard tail, with its tiny yellow daisies.

They had reached the end of the road. Up ahead, in a clearing under scattered cypress trees, sat a whitewashed cabin with a sloped roof, narrow windows and a weathered door. Facing out, a red Cadillac was parked in front of the cabin. Nora didn't mention that it was Lee's. James parked the Buick next to the Cadillac. They both stepped out.

Shielding her eyes with her hands, Nora paused to admire the beauty of Whalers Cove. Directly across from the clearing, she looked down an embankment to an expanse of water surrounded by irregular formations of sedimentary rock on all sides. The iridescent, blue-green water shimmered in the sunlight, as a light breeze pushed up small ripples and stirred tufts of sea grass poking from the rocks.

Nora pulled her sweater around her shoulders and walked down to the narrow beach at the water's edge. She felt peaceful and protected by a land mass of low cliffs to her right, and a high promontory of boulders and shrubbery to her left. She understood why this small, natural harbor offered many a sailor a safe port.

A good distance offshore, two figures frolicked in the kelp bed that floated on top of the water's surface. Nora recognized the one's red-colored bob and the other's lighter blond hair. They were pulling each other under the water and then coming up, laughing. Waving her hand, she called out, "Vera! Lee!" They didn't hear her. Nora kicked off her shoes, shouted at the couple again, and took a few steps into the water. She stopped when she heard James yelling something behind her, but she didn't catch his words.

Apparently, the couple in the water heard him. Nora saw

Vera raise her arms and wave. Then she and Lee plunged forward, their arms stroking through the water as they swam toward shore together. A pair of dolphins, Nora mused.

Pushing her wet hair out of her eyes, Vera stepped from the water first. Lacking a proper bathing costume, her white underskirt was clinging to every contour of her body. She grinned. "Did Annie worry about me and send you two to rescue me?" Her words sounded soft and teasing.

Lee, standing slightly behind her in waist-deep water, was shirtless. His normally pleasant voice that Nora had expected to hear was harsh. "What are you doing out here? Spying on us?"

A squishing sound caused Nora to turn around, just as James bolted past her. She noticed he was carrying a piece of driftwood in his right hand. Rushing up to where Lee was, and using the driftwood like a bat, he struck him on the head and shoulders. Lee fell backwards into the water, swallowed up by the kelp.

Vera screamed and ran.

Throwing the driftwood aside, James chased after her and grabbed her by the arm. Ignoring her cries and her attempts to break free, he picked her up and carried her to his automobile.

Momentarily stunned by what was happening around her, Nora watched the Buick back up and head out of the cove. Turning back, she realized that Lee hadn't surfaced. He might be drowning. Throwing off her sweater, she dove into the water. She shivered and shook off the sudden coldness. Swimming through the beds of kelp, she reached the place where he had gone under. He wasn't there. She guessed he must have drifted farther from shore. Having been a champion swimmer in college, Nora knew that she had the stamina to swim farther out to find him and bring him in. But would she reach Lee in time?

CHAPTER TWENTY EIGHT

After a few quick strokes brought her to where she thought Lee had been, Nora came to an upright position by dog paddling. She looked around and saw the water churning a few yards ahead. He's panicky, she thought. She remembered from her water safety sessions that drowning persons were desperate. They grabbed onto the unwary rescuer, impeded their movements, and dragged them under the water. She had also learned that drowning persons should be approached from the rear — grasp them before they grasp you.

Nora paddled up behind Lee, who had stopped thrashing. His eyes were closed and he was sinking in the water. She thrust her right hand out to reach for the only thing that she could easily grasp — his hair. Pulling his head up, and with his face out of the water, she was able to draw him close to her. Lee offered no resistance. He was unconscious. She then threw her left arm firmly around his upper chest, hooking her hand in his armpit for a good grip, and began kicking vigorously while stroking with her free arm. She headed for the beach.

Minutes later, she dragged his limp body out of the water onto the sand. Rolling him over on one side, she could see the jagged gash on his forehead where James had struck him with the driftwood. She needed to do something to stem the bleeding, but first she had to get him breathing. Bending over him, she pounded on his back, and within seconds, he coughed up mouthfuls of water and gasped several times.

She poked his shoulder. "Take some deep breaths." Tearing off a piece of her underskirt, Nora tied it tightly around his gaping head wound to stem the bleeding. He moaned and fluttered open his eyes.

"Don't worry. You'll be all right," she said, with more conviction than she felt. Already blood had begun to ooze out from under her makeshift bandage. She needed help. Staring at the cabin's shuttered windows, Nora was positive that it wasn't occupied. There was no one around.

She must get Lee out of here quickly if he was going to survive. Just before she and James had taken the road that led to Whalers Cove, she remembered there had been another narrower road running parallel to it. A wooden sign had identified it as the "Allan Toll Road." The name rang a bell. She recalled Annie Stevens saying that, years ago, Mr. Allan and his wife had bought the Point Lobos property for a home and an investment. She had to find out if the Allans had telephone service.

Reaching for her shoes, she slipped them on. She rubbed Lee's hand and said, "I want you to sit up now, and then you're going to stand."

Shaking his head, he mumbled, "Still dizzy."

Helping him to his feet, she slipped her arm around his waist. They slowly walked up the road to where the Cadillac was parked. Nora was relieved to see the key was still in the ignition. She somehow squeezed Lee into the back seat, where she found a blanket. She guessed that he and Vera had spent the night camping out. Getting in on the driver's side, she turned to ask him for instructions, but he was uncommunicative. He was on his side, his shirt collar already bloodstained, and his eyes closed, but breathing. Her first attempt at driving would have to be without his support.

Trying to recall how James had driven from the time they left the filling station, Nora turned the key in the ignition to start the motor, as he had done. She placed her foot on the gas pedal and shifted the hand clutch. She heard a grating sound as the Cadillac lurched and the engine stalled. *What have I forgotten to do?*

Thinking back, she remembered that James had used his left foot on the floor pedal and eased up on it while moving the hand clutch. She tried a second time. The car lurched and again, the motor died. At last, the Cadillac started moving forward.

The road out was a winding one around and under the pine trees. The sun had set and it was getting dark. Nora drove slowly at first and faster as she felt more confident. Finally, reaching the coastal road, she braked, looked in both directions, and made a crawling left turn. Shifting gears, she accelerated until she saw the toll road and turned into it to pull up in front of a wood-framed farm house. She was relieved to see an apron-clad woman sweeping the front porch.

Coming to a stop, Nora shouted, "Are you the lady who is a good friend of Annie Stevens?"

"Yes, I am, miss." The woman stopped sweeping and came out to meet her. She asked, "Who are you, and what's the matter with that young man in the back seat?"

"I'm Nora Finnegan, and he's been badly injured at Whalers Cove. I hope you have a telephone. He needs immediate medical attention."

"We do, young lady, but there's no hospital anywhere around here."

Nora nodded. "There's a very good doctor in Carmel village, so that's where I'm taking him. I would appreciate it, if you would call Annie and have her telephone Doctor Barnes. She needs to let him know that I'm bringing Lee Preston in to see him, and that he has a very serious head wound. Also, would you please ask Annie to contact Marshal Englund and the sheriff? She's to tell them to arrest James Carpenter for assaulting Mr. Preston and leaving him to drown."

"I'll do that right away, Miss Finnegan."

"Thank you very much for your help." Turning the Cadillac in a wide circle, Nora accelerated without stalling the motor and headed back to the coastal road.

Grateful that it wasn't totally dark yet, she drove cautiously. The Cadillac skidded on several curves where there were some patches of loose gravel, but she managed to keep control. Finally, she arrived at the place where the road sloped toward the bridge over the Carmel River. Slowing, she crossed the bridge in a low gear so the bumps wouldn't jar Lee. He had remained silent the whole time.

Coming to a wide intersection where more automobiles were stopping and turning in front of her, she paused to get her bearings. On her right was the turnoff that would take her to Carmel Valley. She knew that the road to her left led to the Carmel Mission. She decided to take it and thereby avoid the hill straight ahead of her and an intimidating challenge, the steep, downhill run on Ocean Avenue into Carmel village.

She turned left when the traffic allowed. Passing the mission church, Nora remembered the last time that she and Lee had been there to attend Sunday mass.

Saying a silent prayer for his recovery, she turned right onto San Carlos Street and headed to the doctor's surgery.

CHAPTER TWENTY NINE

Fortunately, it wasn't dark when Nora reached the outskirts of the village. Since there were no street lights, it would have been a problem. She didn't know how to turn on the Cadillac's headlamps. Having lived in Carmel for nearly a year now, she had no trouble reaching Ninth Avenue. At the corner of Dolores Street, she pulled into a brick driveway next to a large, wood shingled residence whose interior Doctor Barnes had remodeled into his medical clinic and home. He had kept the building's exterior the same as San Francisco architect Willis Polk had designed it twenty years ago.

Two people were waiting for her under the porch light. When they saw her drive up, they headed toward the Cadillac with a medical stretcher.

"I'm glad you made it here without getting into an accident, Miss Finnegan," Doctor Barnes said. "Annie Stevens told me you had never driven before. This is Rose Henderson, my nurse. We'll take over. Just from your passenger's appearance, I can tell that he's suffered a significant blow to his head."

Nora helped them get Lee onto the stretcher and move him inside. She said, "His name is Lee Preston. He has a brother in town. I'll go over and tell Keith what's happened, rather than telephone."

"I'll be happy to speak with him," the doctor said. "Now I suggest you go home and get into some dry clothes."

On the way from Doctor Barnes' surgery, Nora located the switch to the Cadillac's headlights and felt more comfortable driving. It was pitch dark by the time she parked the Cadillac on Monte Verde Street below Keith's log cabin. A light in the window told her that he was at home. Thinking Lee would want his brother to watch over his automobile, she took the keys out of the ignition and ran up the stairs

When he opened the front door, she handed the keys to him. He saw the Cadillac, but not Lee. "Did you find him, Nora? Is he all right?" he blurted.

"Yes, and I'll tell you what happened." He didn't interrupt as she explained James' attack on Lee at Whalers Cove and her drive back to Doctor Barnes' clinic.

"I want to see him," he said, as he grabbed a jacket from a hook by the door. "Did the doctor say he'll recover?"

Nora wasn't sure, but she didn't want to frighten him. "He'll tell you, Keith. I didn't stay long enough to find out."

Lighting his tin lantern, he shut the front door. "Then let's go there now."

"On the way, I'll stop and change my clothes. It will only take me a minute."

Nora and Keith sat together in the doctor's waiting room, while Doctor Barnes was in his surgery taking care of Lee.

Keith said, "For the life of me, I don't know why Carpenter attacked my brother. Do you suppose it was because Lee's play replaced his?"

Nora didn't tell him that she had seen James become furious when he found Lee with Vera. "It might be for that reason. Even in Carmel, actors and playwrights are very competitive people."

Since he had brought up the subject, she decided, as his

good friend, to share her suspicions of Lee's involvement in Guy Porter's poisoning. She said, "I learned that your brother and Vera are longtime friends, Keith. I believe he asked her to do him a favor."

"I never knew that." He listened as she told him about Vera's actions leading up to Porter's death.

When she had finished, he said, "You're saying Vera assaulted Burt Erickson in order to help Lee disrupt Carpenter's play and she put acid in the milk that Porter drank. I can't believe Lee asked her to do all that."

"Yes. He wanted his children's play to be staged this season and Vera helped him accomplish it."

The surgery door opened and Zachary Barnes stepped out. "I have good news," he said. "Your brother has a concussion and he's lost quite a bit of blood. But he will be fine. I sutured his laceration, and he's quite lucid. However, I want to keep him here overnight, so I can check on him and make sure there aren't any complications."

Turning to Nora, he said, "You've been very courageous, Miss Finnegan. Mr. Preston has told me that you saved him from drowning. More than that, you were brave to force yourself to drive an automobile for the first time in your life. He certainly would have died if you hadn't been there to rescue him. He and his family owe you a great deal of thanks."

"That's absolutely true, Doctor," Keith chimed in. "I'm in Miss Finnegan's debt and so will my parents be, as soon as I telephone them." Getting to his feet, he picked up his tin lantern and lit the candle inside. "Now why don't I escort you home, Nora? Then I'll come back to stay with Lee until he's well enough to leave. I'll return shortly, Doc."

Keith took Nora's arm as they walked down Ninth and turned at the corner of Monte Verde Street.

"Perhaps Lee and I ought to take a trip to see our parents

when he's fully recovered," Keith said. "It might be good for him to get away from Carmel for a while."

"Before you make any plans, I believe the sheriff will want to talk to him, to find out where he was early Saturday morning at the time Guy Porter died."

Keith remained silent. When he finally looked at her, even in the lantern's dim light, Nora could see that he was smiling.

"My brother didn't have anything to do with Porter's death, and here's why. Last Friday night, after leaving your place, we drove out to Egan's roadhouse. I'm afraid I had a few too many ciders. I could hardly stand up and I became sick as a dog. Lee drove me home and said that I shouldn't be alone. He spent the entire night at the cabin with me, holding my head over the toilet most of the time. He didn't leave until he came to pick you up to go to your softball practice, Nora. He was nowhere near Guy Porter when he was murdered."

CHAPTER THIRTY

Nora was glad to get home. Every muscle in her body ached from rescuing Lee in the cove, plus the nervous strain of driving from Point Lobos back to Carmel. She said to Keith, "Thanks for seeing me home. I'll meet you in the morning at Doctor Barnes' surgery."

"I'll be staying there all night, and again, a heartfelt thank you, for what you did for Lee today, Nora."

Opening Pine Log's front gate, Nora said goodnight and headed along the side path to her back door. She was looking forward to a hot bath and ten hours of uninterrupted sleep. Softball practice tomorrow morning was out of the question, but she would get to the *Pine Cone* office at noon. She and Mr. Owens had to make their weekly rounds of the village merchants and advertisers. As much as she looked forward to learning all aspects of the newspaper business, she wished she could cancel.

Stooping down, she lifted a clay pot filled with succulents and retrieved her house key. About to step inside, she heard what sounded like a car door slam shut. Turning around, she was surprised to see Sheriff Connery striding up the path.

"Was that Lee Preston's brother you were walking with?" he called out.

Nora winced. "Wouldn't it have been better if you had

started the conversation with, 'Good evening, Miss Finnegan. How are you holding up after such a trying day?'"

Jimmy sighed. "How about asking me how my day went? I'd much rather be relaxing at home, reading a book to Molly. Instead, I'm standing out here in the cold."

"I see you decided to stop by and talk to me in person instead of calling me. Is that so I won't hang up on you when I don't like your attitude?" When he didn't respond, she said, "Well, come on in, but make it brief. Mrs. Newsom has already spotted your police sedan by now, and she'll have some interesting gossip to share with our neighbors at the milk shrine tomorrow morning if you stay too long."

He muttered something under his breath that she didn't hear and followed her inside.

Hanging up her sweater on a hook by the door, Nora kicked off her shoes and motioned him to join her in the kitchen. The bath would have to wait, but she was starving, and not about to make any pretense of being a good hostess. She went to the bread box, removed a half-eaten loaf of bread, and took a bottle of milk from the icebox. He could watch her eat while he told her why he was here.

They both sat down at the kitchen table. Like two cats waiting to pounce, each waited for the other to make the first move. Nora cut off several pieces of bread and said, "There's some milk left in the bottle if you care to join me."

He got up and found a clean glass in her cupboard. After pouring out a small amount, he sat back down. Taking a sip, he said, "I can see by your eyes how exhausted you are, Nora, but there are several good reasons why I came to see you in person, rather than telephoning. It's important that I take care of this tonight. It's about the Porter murder case."

"Did you get a warrant to search Vera's room at Annie Stevens' lodge?"

Jimmy leaned back in his chair and rolled his eyes. "Not only did I do that, Miss Finnegan, but I spoke to Burt Erickson, who substantiated what you had already told me. Also, when Annie conveyed your message to Marshal Englund that James Carpenter had nearly killed Lee Preston at Point Lobos, the marshal called me immediately and we went together to Carpenter's home. We found Miss Winfield there with him. After arresting them on charges of aggravated assault, I had the marshal drive them to jail in Monterey. That gave me time to come here to talk to you. Deputy Jensen is booking them now and putting them into separate holding cells."

"I'm glad they're both in custody. Vera seems sweet and vulnerable at first, but I've come to realize she is a very manipulative woman. On the other hand, I was very surprised to find out what an uncontrollable temper James Carpenter has."

"Actually, that's why I'm here tonight. I need a sworn statement from you as a witness to his attack on Lee Preston."

Nora nodded. "His brother Keith and I just came from seeing Lee at Doctor Barnes' surgery. From what the doctor said, Lee will probably be well enough to talk to you tomorrow. Is there anything else I can do before you leave, Jimmy?"

"Yes, there is one more thing. When we took Miss Winfield into custody, she became hysterical. She's insisting that she will only confess to what she did if you're there to report her side of the story. Marshal Englund thinks that today's events unnerved her. She claims that Preston and Carpenter will put all the blame on her, including the murder of Guy Porter."

"That's fine. I can be there, but only if you promise to give me the exclusive story for my newspaper. If you agree, then I'll telephone Mr. Owens and let him know what you've asked me to do. I'll go to Keith's cabin tomorrow morning, where I left Lee's Cadillac, and drive it to the jail in Monterey."

Jimmy reached out his hand and took hers. "I can't allow

that, Nora."

"What are you talking about?"

He chuckled. "Without a document issued by the California Division of Motor Vehicles stating that you have a paid permit to drive a car, I'd have to arrest you."

Getting up from his chair, he walked over to the sink and put his glass down on the counter. Looking back at her, he said, "I've overstayed my welcome. I'll stop by for you in the morning. Say nine o'clock."

"Can I ask you something before you go, Jimmy? And promise me that you won't be irked."

"Are you going to be sweet and manipulative like Vera Winfield?"

She shrugged him off. "You and I collaborated on a prior murder case last year and I recall that your deputy, Alvin Jensen, had mastered the technique of fingerprinting."

"That's true, and since I've been sheriff, I instituted a new policy that everyone we arrest has to have their fingerprints taken first thing. Were you going to remind me to take Miss Winfield's prints?"

"Well, I was only thinking that if her fingerprints match those on the milk bottle I found at the Forest Theater, she becomes your prime suspect for Porter's murder."

"I'm way ahead of you, Nora. I also think Lee Preston is involved in that crime. We'll make sure to get his fingerprints too."

"Then I think you will have a problem."

"What do you mean?"

"Lee's brother Keith is going to provide him with an alibi."

Jimmy shook his head. "If you didn't already have a job, I would ask you to work for me."

"I wouldn't last long, Sheriff. I don't think we would be compatible."

CHAPTER THIRTY ONE

Saturday

Unable to sleep, Nora had risen early and dressed. By seven o'clock, she had walked to the corner milk shrine, picked up her pint bottle of milk, and returned to make breakfast. On most Saturdays, she would have hiked out to Carmel Point for her softball team's weekly practice. Today would be different.

Opening her door, she stepped off the back porch and took in a deep breath. No morning fog. The sun was shining brightly. She looked up at the roof-high Norfolk Island pine that was planted by her parents when they first bought the place as a vacation home years ago. The tree had become the centerpiece attraction of her small back yard.

She loved living here in Carmel, despite all the terrible things that had happened this past week. As a reporter, her mind had become preoccupied with the news stories they generated. Guy Porter, the lead actor in a play that she had a small part in, had been murdered in his upstairs bedroom at Annie Stevens' boarding house. The case was not solved. Two people she had considered friends, Vera Winfield and James Carpenter, had been arrested, one as a possible murder suspect, and the other for assault with intent to murder someone else. They were both in jail. So was

Victor Wolfe, Porter's understudy, for bribing Tommy Anderson with the intent of injuring, and then replacing the play's leading man, Porter. Lee Preston, her friend Keith's brother, had almost drowned at Whalers Cove if she hadn't been there to save him. Lee too had a hidden agenda for being in Carmel.

In the span of one year, her job as a news reporter had become her life. She had been right by deciding to turn down Jimmy's offer of marriage. Now she was about to write her first exclusive news story on a well-publicized murder case, something she knew she would prize later in life.

Looking up into a nearby pine's uppermost branches, she saw a pair of crows staring down at her. For once they didn't make their noisy cawing sound, but merely hopped from branch to branch. She thought that their life was probably less stressed than hers. It was time to leave for Doctor Barnes' clinic.

Keith was waiting for her on the doctor's front porch steps. He got up and said, "Lee's feeling much better this morning, thank God."

They met the nurse at the door and were ushered into Lee's room. He was in a metal hospital bed, a clean bandage on his head with no blood seepage. He raised his eyebrows to open his eyes. Both were partially swollen. The upper and lower lids had turned a shade of dark blue, almost black, in color.

Nora couldn't help but smile. He looked like a raccoon. She took a seat in a chair next to the bed. "How are you, Lee?"

Nurse Henderson spoke up. "He's had a light breakfast, and seems much more alert today. I'll let the doctor know you're here, Miss Finnegan."

"I want to thank you, Nora," Lee said. "You saved my life yesterday and I'll never forget it."

"I'm glad I could. Has the sheriff come by to see you this morning?"

"No, he hasn't. Why should he?" He looked over at his brother. "I've done nothing wrong. I was the victim."

Keith shook his head. Without looking at his brother, he walked over to an open window and looked out at the garden behind the clinic. In a low voice, he said, "Nora believes you paid Vera to get rid of Guy Porter, in order to shut down Carpenter's play."

Sitting up, Lee's face turned red with anger. "Why would you believe her, a perfect stranger, instead of your own brother? Look at me, Keith."

Keith didn't turn around, but continued staring out the window. "Nora's not a stranger. She's a good friend and I believe her. I've come to know her far better than I ever knew you." Returning to the side of his bed, he looked down at his brother. "Vera was blackmailing you, wasn't she, Lee? That's why you needed to empty our trust fund, so you could pay her off. She's a schemer, but you're worse. You've embarrassed the family name, not to mention me. Why did I encourage you to come here? I'm the town's librarian and I have a good reputation, not to mention reliable friends like Nora. I hope you'll be punished for what you did and go to jail."

Nora intervened, "Calm down, Keith. But you're right. It does matter if Lee paid Vera to do some bad things. Maybe he didn't pull out the breathing tube so that Guy suffocated, but the sheriff is looking to charge him as Vera's accomplice. Turning to Lee, she added, "You don't know it, but he's already arrested her."

Lee's face paled. "All right. I admit I gave Vera money to buy clothes and expensive trinkets. But they were simply gifts, not bribes to do evil things. I'm pleading with you to help me, Nora. You have influence with this sheriff. I've seen how he looks at you. Get him to believe me."

"How dare you suggest such a thing, Lee Preston! When are you going to tell your brother the truth about why you asked for the money in yours and Keith's trust fund? You couldn't have given all twenty-five thousand dollars to Vera."

"What do you mean?"

Nora stood up. "I made a telephone call to the publicist at your Hollywood studio. I found out your real motive for coming here. I don't think it's going to sit well with the directors of the Forest Theater when they learn what you were up to. Nor will it please Edward Kuster. You misrepresented yourself to him."

"I have no idea what you're talking about."

"Then let me explain. I want Keith to hear this too. The publicist I spoke with told me that you were hired by a movie syndicate to travel to small towns like Carmel and convince their leaders to allow the building of new theaters on their main streets where films could be shown. That's probably why you bought your new Cadillac."

Lee snickered. "That's absolutely ridiculous!"

"Is it? The Hollywood studios are expecting a huge surge in business in the near future with talkies. A Palo Alto inventor by the name of DeForest is currently experimenting with sound-on-film movies. I think you intended to use your family trust money to invest in Edward Kuster's proposed theater on Ocean Avenue. Your goal is to have your syndicate control the theater to show your movie studio's films and maybe phase out play productions entirely. You're betting that venues like the Forest Theater and the proposed Arts and Crafts Club Theater are going to be obsolete and disappear. When Mr. Kuster returns to Carmel, I think he will be very angry about your secret plan. He has written to Mr. Owens that his theater will be an all-Carmel institution run by local people."

Lee's face darkened. "You can't prove any of this."

"I'll get Sheriff Connery to do that by giving him my Hollywood source and he can pursue it. And perhaps Vera has some interesting information about you to tell the sheriff. By the way, I left your Cadillac at Keith's place. I don't think I'll be having you teach me how to drive."

Getting up, Nora walked out, and left the two brothers to deal with their problems. As she came into the clinic's waiting room, she met Doctor Barnes.

"I see you've come to visit Lee," he said. "He can be discharged this afternoon. By the way, I hope we still have that date for a hike on the beach tomorrow."

The anger that she had just experienced in the other room melted away. Zachary Barnes seemed like a decent man, one who wouldn't deceive her. Smiling up at him, she said, "I'm looking forward to it, Doctor Barnes. And I'm planning on packing us a picnic lunch."

"It's Zach. And I hope you'll allow me to call you Nora."

"See you at the Bath House at two o'clock, Zach." As she closed the surgery's front door, Nora knew why people always felt better after they talked to a doctor.

CHAPTER THIRTY TWO

Sunday

Nora threw off the quilt and slipped out of bed to face the morning. What had she done? The first thought that popped into her head wasn't about her exclusive story of Vera Winfield's emotional admission of guilt yesterday afternoon at the Monterey jail. It was about her impulsive promise to prepare a picnic lunch for Doctor Barnes today.

Silly, of course, but it was worrisome nonetheless. She hardly knew the doctor, which meant she had no idea what to cook for him. More important, what had prompted her to accept his invitation? There was no way of getting out of it.

First things first. Only one person had the culinary expertise she needed — a woman who would get her through this crisis of her own making. Putting on her robe, she headed to the front room and picked up the telephone. She asked the operator for a San Francisco number.

"Hello. Finnegan residence," her mother said.

"How are you this morning, Mother?" As she asked the question, Nora realized that the last time she had spoken to either of her parents had been a couple of weeks ago.

"We were just discussing you over dinner last night, Nora. You really must call us more often. William Owens telephoned your father yesterday and mentioned this recent murder case in Carmel. He said things were fairly hectic at the *Pine Cone* and that you've been working long hours to cover the story. I'm hoping you're not neglecting your social life and devoting all your time to your job."

"That's part of the reason I'm calling. I need advice from an older woman."

"I'm always happy to counsel you, dear."

"Yes, I know you are, but in this case, I don't need that kind of advice. Is Mrs. Simon there?"

"What do you want to talk to her about?"

"Baking."

"Well, I know that's not my department. Hold on, and I'll get her."

Nora had known Helen Simon, the Finnegans' longtime housekeeper and cook since childhood. A widow, she was more like a family member than an employee.

When she came on the line, Helen said, "I've missed you, Nora. How are you?"

"I've missed you as well, and especially now. I'm fixing a picnic for a male friend and trying a neighbor's recipe for strawberry shortcake for the first time. Can you guide me through the steps of making it?"

Laughing, Helen said, "That's easy. Do you have some baking soda in your pantry?"

"Hold on a minute." Checking the kitchen cupboard, she found a small metal tin with the words, "Baking Powder" on one side. She had no idea how long it had been there, but it had never been opened. Returning to the telephone, she said, "Will baking powder do?"

"Either soda or powder will be fine. Now read off the list of ingredients that you have on your recipe."

"There's flour, sugar, salt, butter, milk and eggs."

"That's perfect."

For the next few minutes, Nora took careful notes on how to blend the dry ingredients, cut in the butter, and mix everything together.

"Be sure to moisten the batter with just the right amount of milk," Helen said. "Use a tablespoon to drop the shortcakes onto a baking sheet. You'll know they're cooked when a toothpick comes out clean."

"It sounds complicated, but not impossible," Nora said, as she wrote everything down. "I'll give you a full report on how they turn out."

'I'm sure you'll do just fine, and remember, men love quantity, not quality. Fill him with food and he'll think you're a good cook."

"Thank you, Helen, and please don't say anything to Mother about this."

"My lips are sealed, child."

Nora returned to the kitchen and assembled what she needed. She followed the recipe exactly. Then she lit the oven and put the shortcakes in. While waiting for them to bake, she sliced and sugared a pint of fresh strawberries she had purchased yesterday at Leidig's grocery store and set them aside in a covered bowl. She hoped Doctor Barnes wouldn't mind not having whipped cream ladled on top. There probably was some way to fix it for a picnic, but she had forgotten to ask Helen.

Thankfully, her neighbor, Mrs. Newsom, had left half a roasted chicken at the back door last night. Taking it out of the icebox, she cut it into good-sized pieces and placed them in a covered pan. In a bowl, she mixed some coarsely chopped leftover boiled potatoes with diced celery, added shelled and sliced hardboiled eggs, then some mayonnaise, salt and pepper. Meanwhile, the shortcakes were done.

Getting out her mother's wicker picnic basket, she put the heaviest items on the bottom, then two bottles of root beer, dishes and some utensils wrapped up in napkins. There was just enough room to slide in half a dozen shortcakes stowed in a paper bag. When she was finished, Nora gave a big sigh of relief, looked out the kitchen window, and was delighted to see that the sun was shining brightly.

In the bedroom she put on a lightweight middy blouse and decided on a loose fitting pleated skirt that would make the hiking part of the picnic more comfortable. Wearing her broad-brimmed hat to ward off the sun, she picked up her basket and headed out the back door to meet Zachary Barnes.

Thankfully, the trip was downhill to the beach, because the picnic basket became heavier as she walked. The doctor was waiting for her at the end of Ocean Avenue next to the Bath House. A blanket was rolled up under his arm. She had never seen him informally dressed. He wore a pair of tan-colored trousers and a short-sleeved white shirt open at the throat. For the first time, Nora saw him as quite an attractive man.

"Hello, Zach," she called out. "Have I kept you waiting?"

"No. I just got here. Let me help you with that heavy basket." He reached over and took it from her. "Something smells delicious."

"I hope you like it. Here, give me the blanket. You shouldn't have to carry it too." She led the way to a sand dune shaded by a tall, bushy cypress tree and spread out the blanket under it. Having overcome her concerns about fixing the food, and noticing the friendly demeanor of the doctor, Nora was prepared to enjoy the outing. She even fantasized that this picnic might not be their last.

"I couldn't eat another bite," Zach said. "Everything

was delicious, Nora. You're a very good cook, and even better company."

"I'm glad you were hungry, so we don't have to take home any leftovers."

"I can't remember when I ate so much. It was all good, especially your strawberry shortcake."

"That's kind of you to say, Zach." She didn't think she had to tell him it was her first attempt at baking anything.

He got to his feet and stretched. "Why don't I stow the blanket and your basket behind the Bath House. I want to show you a spot that I think you'll appreciate as much as I did when I first hiked there last month."

Jumping up, Nora said, "That sounds interesting. I'd like to see it."

It was low tide and a cooling sea breeze was blowing. They moved along the beach and turned to climb a low hill dotted with coastal live oaks and pine trees. He stopped a few feet ahead of her and pointed at a grouping of colorful shrubs in an open area located a short distance off the trail.

Somehow, it felt pleasant to be shown something that he found remarkable, she thought.

"What do you think, Nora? I found out that these native plants are called monkey-flowers. I'm glad they're still blooming, so I can show them to you."

She observed the waist-high, flowering plants with their apricot-colored blossoms. They were quite lovely, but what was even more impressive to her was the sensitive side of the man next to her. She said, "You're right. This is a special place. Thank you for sharing it with me. I'll always remember it."

"Since moving here, I've come to appreciate the natural beauty of the area around Carmel. It's quite a change from having lived in cities on the east coast."

"I've had a similar experience, having grown up in San

Francisco and going to college in Oakland."

"We have a lot in common. I've lived most of my life in Boston, and attended medical school in Philadelphia."

"I've never been east, but I know that part of the country has seasonal weather."

He nodded. "Yes. As a youngster, I enjoyed my winter sports of skiing and ice hockey, and I learned to tolerate the hot summers. The west coast is unique, with its year-long, temperate climate. I feel privileged to be living here and meeting friendly people like you."

"How do you like practicing medicine in a small town? With your training, my guess is that you were invited to join doctors' practices in large cities or even stay and teach in the medical school."

"That life didn't appeal to me. I wanted to do something different. When I found out that there was an opening as a family practitioner here, I took it. I have no regrets." He hesitated. "Well, that isn't exactly true."

"What do you mean?"

Zachary Barnes looked down. "I've had my first patient death here. That's a terrible thing for a doctor starting out in practice. When I came to Mrs. Stevens' lodge in the middle of the night a week ago, I was able to do an emergency tracheotomy. I was excited to have saved Guy Porter's life by doing that. I knew he would improve by morning. In time, his throat swelling would subside and he would be able to breathe on his own. Maybe he might have residual scarring and his voice might be different, but Guy Porter would be alive."

"It wasn't your fault that he died," Nora said. "Someone else didn't want him to survive." Having developed the habit of posing questions as a reporter, she asked in a matter-of-fact manner, "Was there anything unusual about the night you went to see Mr. Porter — anything that might point to who killed him?"

"You know, I never thought about it much until now, but I did notice something odd on my way home from the lodge. There was an automobile parked under the trees nearby, with someone sitting at the wheel. I should have wondered who would be out at four-thirty in the morning. I've made enough night house calls around here to know that Carmelites are in bed at that hour. I guess I should have mentioned what I saw to Marshal Englund."

"Can you describe the vehicle, Zach?"

When Doctor Barnes did, Nora knew immediately who had run up Annie Stevens' stairs in the middle of the night to pull out Guy Porter's breathing tube.

CHAPTER THIRTY THREE

Monday

Walking out of his office, William Owens noticed Nora and Mary Lee standing at the counter in the *Pine Cone*'s reception area. As he approached the front, he could hear them laughing. He said, "What's so funny, ladies?"

His wife smiled at him. "A minute ago, I transferred an urgent telephone call to Nora from her young friend, Freddie. I could hardly understand the boy, he was speaking so rapidly. Nora just told me what he was so excited about."

Owens frowned. "What did young Jacklin want, Honora?"

Nora chuckled. "He called to tell me about an earthshaking event that occurred at his house. It concerns the Cavalier King Charles spaniel I gave him last November — the one who desperately needed a home. You remember Maisie, don't you, Mr. Owens?"

"How could I forget her? She caused so much mischief around this office for weeks on end. Between her and our dog's antics, we didn't have a moment's peace." Shaking his head, he added, "I was so relieved when you found her a good home with the Jacklins so Mary Lee and I didn't have to keep her. We already have Dasher."

Hearing his name, the Owens' dog let out a loud bark. Mary Lee looked down at the Welsh corgi lying at her feet. "You know who Maisie is, don't you, boy? It's been no fun around here. I'm sure you'd like some four-legged company."

Ignoring his wife's veiled suggestion that they should get a second dog, Owens said to Nora, "So what was Freddie's big news?"

"Maisie had a litter of puppies last night, and all three of them are fine, healthy specimens. Freddie wants to know if you and Mrs. Owens would like to adopt one. He expressly said that you would have your pick of the litter."

"Don't you dare, Mary Lee!" Owens exclaimed. "One mutt is all I can take. But I'm forgetting why I came out here. Holding up several pieces of paper, he said, "I just finished reading Honora's interview with Vera Winfield. I didn't change a word of the text. You did a superb job capturing the young woman's story. Good work!"

Nora beamed. "Thank you, Mr. Owens."

"I've been dying to read it too," Mary Lee said. "Answering the telephone keeps me busy, but it's quieted down a bit this morning and I have the time."

Owens handed her the story.

Nora was anxious to get a woman's opinion on Vera Winfield's confession.

ACTRESS CONFESSES TO ASSAULT — NOT MURDER

Vera Winfield, a twenty-five-year-old stage and motion picture actress, was taken into police custody last Friday evening from the Carmel home of James Carpenter. The arresting officers were Monterey County Sheriff, James Connery, and Marshal Gus Englund of Carmel-By-The-Sea. The charges lodged by the sheriff against Miss Winfield include two counts of assault with intent to incur great bodily harm. These events occurred at the Forest Theater a week ago on Friday evening. The actress is also suspected of the murder of Guy Porter, the leading actor in a play that was in rehearsal at the theater. In Miss Winfield's own words, as obtained in an exclusive interview with the *Carmel Pine Cone*, she admits to the crimes of assault, but vigorously denies committing the murder. Below is her personal narrative of what occurred, according to Miss Winfield.

"My name is Vera Winfield. I was born and grew up in in Santa Monica, California, where I was exposed to the world of acting during my high school days. That early experience caused me to follow a path that led first to the film studios in Hollywood as an actress in the movies, and from there, to San Francisco, where I found acting work on the professional stage. While in Hollywood, I made the acquaintance of Lee Preston, a screenwriter whom I came to know well. He introduced me to many directors who furthered my career. He found acting roles for me in the movies, as well as in stage plays. So it was no surprise when, early this year, Mr. Preston contacted me to help him gain access to the theater world in Carmel. He asked me to help him shut down a play being directed by James Carpenter at the Forest Theater. That would allow his play to take its place. Since I was an understudy to the play's leading actress, familiar with the staging and the actions of the play, as well as knowing the play's cast and crew, I agreed to help Mr. Preston accomplish his goal. I felt obligated to return the favors he did for me by helping me get my career started. Mr. Preston and I concocted a scheme whereby I was to disable the play's prop man to prevent him from preparing a tea tray that was used in the play's first act. Once he was unable to do his job, I was to put a non-lethal amount of muriatic acid in a pitcher of milk that Guy Porter would add to his tea during rehearsal. It was Mr. Preston who suggested the acid. He said it would only cause some burning in Mr. Porter's throat. I never would have agreed to do this if I knew it would kill him.

How did you get the muriatic acid?

It so happened that a man who was building a wall at the lodge where I live was storing acid in my landlady's back yard. I admit striking Burt Erickson, the elderly prop man with a piece of kindling. Then, when he was knocked out, I took the tea tray and added milk and a small amount of acid to the pitcher. My intent was to injure Guy Porter's voice, so that the play would be delayed, and hopefully, cancelled. What I did was reprehensible, but I strenuously deny trying to murder him. He was a friend of mine.

Did Mr. Preston provide you with any incentives to do these things?

Yes. Mr. Preston paid me five hundred dollars. I needed it because I wasn't earning much money at my part-time sales job. I owed my landlady three months back rent, so the cash came in handy. Mr. Preston also gave me numerous gifts.

Did Mr. Preston ever threaten you?

After Mr. Porter was murdered at the boarding house where I stay, I wanted to confess my participation in this unexpected tragedy, but I was threatened by a Hollywood friend of Mr. Preston's. He frightened me into saying nothing. That happened at Egan's place in Carmel Valley. From then on, I was very afraid of what might happen to me if I didn't do what Mr. Preston wanted me to do or if I went to the sheriff and told him what I did. I can't prove who killed Guy Porter. I just know that I didn't. I'll leave that up to the sheriff to figure out. I hope that people who read this account of my actions won't judge me too harshly. I always wanted to be an actress and I still do, but I know now that it is a very competitive business, and it's not as glamorous as it seems."

When she had finished reading Nora's story, Mary Lee looked up and said, "Excellent reporting."

CHAPTER THIRTY FOUR

Nora and Jimmy were seated at one of the Blue Bird's tables for two. Both had ordered the tea room's daily lunch special of grilled ham and cheese sandwiches on rye. Nora picked up the Chintzware pot and poured out two cups of steaming tea.

Leaning forward and straightening his sheriff's badge, Jimmy said, "This seems like old times. When you called me at home last night to tell me who had murdered Guy Porter, I told you once again to stop meddling in police business. And I meant it."

Nora bristled. "You also said that you had solved the case, and that you would give me the official story for my newspaper only over lunch today. That's when I decided I wouldn't share what I knew until now. Two can play that childish game."

"I believe you were the one who slammed down the telephone, not me. So who was being childish, Nora? Anyway, I figured that we both have to eat lunch, and the Blue Bird is as public a place as any in Carmel." Taking a sip of his tea, he nodded at Marshal Gus Englund, who was sitting with two of the town's elected officials at a table by the front window.

"This has been a difficult week for both of us, Jimmy. Shall we call a truce? And while we wait for our lunch to arrive, why don't I tell you what I know."

Folding his arms across his chest, he said, "I'm listening."

She had no intention of providing him with the details of yesterday's picnic when she had obtained Zachary Barnes' revealing information. Instead, she decided only to recount what the doctor had seen in the early morning hours last Saturday outside Annie Stevens' lodge. "Doctor Barnes described James Carpenter's blue sedan, with him in the front seat, parked near the entrance. As I listened to him, I immediately recognized who owned the Buick." She paused to pour more tea to give her words more significance. "You see, I was a passenger in that car on our ride to Point Lobos. I remembered during play rehearsals that James became very upset over Vera's flirtations with Guy Porter, not to mention how angry he must have been because of their daily proximity to each other in Annie's boarding house. When he and I saw Vera and Lee together at Whalers Cove, something must have snapped inside him."

"I wasn't aware that Carpenter was jealous of other men's attentions to Vera."

"James told me that he planned to marry her. So now that I've supplied you with his motive for Porter's murder, one that you didn't have, why don't you tell me how you solved the case?"

"A motive is always helpful, but in this murder case, we needed more evidence than that. I have it. Utilizing the latest police technology, we've been able to confirm that Carpenter was the killer. Deputy Jensen has identified his bloody fingerprints on Doctor Barnes' tracheotomy tube."

The news surprised Nora. "But why weren't the doctor's prints on the tube?"

"That's because he used surgical gloves when he inserted it. Gloves don't leave prints. Just to show you how effective fingerprint technology is, we were also able to find Miss Winfield's prints on the milk bottle she discarded at the theater before your play rehearsal started. That confirms that she mixed the acid into the milk. It took Deputy Jensen a little time to process all the fingerprints after we arrested both of them Saturday night. When I spoke with you, I wasn't being childish. I just needed a little more time before telling you."

The waitress arrived with their food. Before taking a bite of her sandwich, Nora said, "It seems to me that many men have trouble dealing with jealousy."

"I know you're implying something personal, and I admit that I've been jealous when I've seen you with other men."

From his tone, Nora wondered if their future professional relationship would be more strained. She would have to wait and see. "I want to thank you for giving me this breaking news on the murder," she said. "It will be on the front page of the *Pine Cone* on Wednesday morning. Mr. Owens is also going to run my jail interview with Vera Winfield. I'll make sure to add the fact that, while you found her fingerprints on the milk bottle, she isn't a murderess."

"Just so you know, I'll be presenting the evidence against her and Carpenter to the District Attorney on Wednesday." Jimmy paused to pour them more tea. "It must have been quite an ordeal to rescue Lee Preston at Whalers Cove. The man owes his life to you."

Nora noticed that his compliment was sincere, his voice soothing and pleasant. It brought back memories of a friendlier and more intimate time. She pushed away the feeling.

"By the way, are you going to arrest Lee as Vera's accomplice in her crime?"

"I don't think so. We found only one set of fingerprints on the milk bottle. They were Vera's. I questioned Preston extensively at his brother's cabin yesterday. As far as Vera's claim that he paid her money and bought her expensive gifts to do his bidding, he told me that he was just helping her out as an old friend."

"Did he admit that he suggested she poison Porter with acid?"

"Yes, but he said it was only a joke. Moreover, he said that he never told his Hollywood friend or anyone else to harm her. He claims that everyone knows Vera's a flirt who enjoys teasing men and leading them on."

"You're saying that you don't have any solid proof that Lee committed a crime?"

He nodded. "It's only Vera's word against his. Before I left him, he said that he was returning to Hollywood, as long as I wasn't going to arrest him. Apparently, the Forest Theater Society has cancelled all plays for the rest of the year, Preston's included. I'll stay in touch with him though. I told him that he has to come back here as a material witness for the trials. He's agreed to do so."

"Thank you for sharing your information with me, Jimmy. It's going to be very satisfying for my paper to beat out our Monterey competitor. I hope you'll keep me in mind whenever any future news story concerning Carmel comes up."

He nodded, but didn't say anything.

She thought he seemed sad. Looking up at the cuckoo clock on the far wall, she said, "And thanks for my lunch. I should get back to work so that Mr. Owens can start typesetting these additions to my stories."

Jimmy stood up and signaled their waitress for the bill. Looking down at Nora, he said, "I can see why you wouldn't marry me. You're already married to your job."

As they were walking out, they met Doc Staniford at the Blue Bird's front door.

Tipping his hat, the druggist said, "Afternoon, folks. Did you hear that I caught my burglar red-handed? I was working after hours last night and witnessed the whole thing."

Taking out her notepad and pencil, Nora asked, "May I have the details, Doc?"

"No need to write anything down," the druggist said. "And

you won't have to arrest anyone, Sheriff."

Jimmy looked puzzled. "Why is that?"

"It turns out Archie was the interloper. He's the cat that lives in the shop next to my drugstore. He's kept inside at night to catch my neighbor's mice, but Archie found his way into my place through an open window last Thursday evening. He must have jumped up on the shelf of glass beakers where I had stored the muriatic acid specimen Marshal Englund gave me to analyze. The darned cat knocked them all to the floor. And he broke half a dozen more last night, after I had replaced the original ones."

Nora grinned. "In the future, you'll have to make sure all your windows are closed, Doc, or move the beakers somewhere else." Looking at Jimmy, she added, "I bet Sheriff Connery wishes that all of his burglaries were as easy to solve as yours was."

Jimmy smiled. "Case closed, Nora. This is one you won't have to investigate."

CHAPTER THIRTY FIVE

Sunday, August 27, 1922

Nora had been up since six in the morning, cleaning her cottage from top to bottom. As she worked, she wished she had her mother's housekeeper to help her, if only for the weekend. At eight, her friend Keith Preston arrived with two library tables in the back of Pete Quinlan's truck. The two men carried them down Nora's driveway to the back yard and set them up like long refectory tables under the Norfolk Island pine.

Once they departed, Nora dusted the front room thoroughly, cleaned the kitchen and bath, and picked up a couple of throw rugs. Stepping out onto her front porch, she hoped that anyone walking home from services at the nearby Episcopal Church wouldn't be shocked at seeing her shake them out. Expecting a houseful of guests at two o'clock this afternoon, she had a good excuse for cleaning her cottage on a Sunday.

"Nora? Are you busy?" Lucinda Newsom called out from her kitchen window. "I need you to help me bring over the food I've prepared. Some of it needs to be kept cold until later."

Bringing in the throw rugs, Nora hurried across their shared driveway to her neighbor's cottage. Together, they carried covered containers of food from the Newsom kitchen into Nora's. The beef roast with potatoes and a variety of vegetables were placed in the oven to keep warm, while the salads went into the icebox.

When they had finished, Lucinda poked around Nora's cottage and then stepped out onto the back porch. She said, "Everything looks spotless. Now don't worry about getting the food in the bowls and on platters after your guests arrive. I'll be over to help you with that."

Nora gave her a big hug. "You've done so much for me, Mrs. Newsom. You're a wonderful neighbor and friend."

At one-thirty, Nora was busy wiping water spots off two crystal vases when she heard someone step up on the front porch.

Claudia Jacklin shouted through the open half of the Dutch door, "It's me, Nora."

Coming into the front room, Nora saw that her friend's arms encircled a large bunch of cut flowers. "Let me take those from you," she said, as she opened the lower half of the door. "They're lovely, Claudia. Come into the kitchen. I have some vases for those roses from your garden. I'll use them as centerpieces on the tables in the back yard. And you're just in time to help me."

Claudia followed Nora down the back steps. Brushing her hair away from her perspiring face, she sat down heavily on one of the benches that Keith and Pete had put alongside the tables.

Nora bent over and gave her friend a pat on the shoulder. "What was I thinking? I forgot about your condition. You look absolutely beautiful, Claudia. Pregnancy certainly agrees with you. And that's a lovely new frock you're wearing."

"Thanks. It fits perfectly now, but it won't in a month or so. Doctor Barnes thinks I may be having twins." She laughed. "Have your parents and Mrs. Simon arrived yet?"

"They're at the hotel. The three of them took the train from

San Francisco and arrived yesterday. They have two lovely rooms on the Pine Inn's top floor. Mother telephoned a while ago and offered to come early and help me today, but I assured her that you and I have everything under control. We do, don't we?"

Wiping her brow with a lace handkerchief, Claudia smiled. "Of course we do. Aren't we capable, twentieth century women?" She stood up and smoothed the wrinkles on her dress. "Just how many guests are you expecting?"

"I invited seventeen adults, including you and me, plus two children."

"I know this is a surprise party to celebrate your parents' twenty-fifth wedding anniversary, but I had no idea so many people were coming."

"Mother and Father were married here in Carmel. They love the place. I wanted to do something special for them and the guest list just grew."

Nora had worked on the seating arrangements for the past month. Her parents, Alice and John Finnegan, and their oldest friends, the *Carmel Pine Cone*'s publisher, William Owens and his wife, Mary Lee, would be seated together at one of the tables. Also there would be the Finnegans' good friends, Henry Preston and his wife, Cora. Every summer, Keith's parents traveled from Charleston, South Carolina to Carmel for a visit. Nora had telephoned them and they had been delighted to make the trip now. In addition to the three couples, Nora planned to seat Helen Simon, the Finnegan's housekeeper, and Lucinda Newsom, their longtime Carmel neighbor, at her parents' table.

When she had learned that Doctor Zachary Barnes' parents would also be in town, Nora had happily included them. Mark and Lila Barnes had been eager to see their son's new location. They, and Zach's older sister, Patricia, had arrived from Boston a week ago. Nora had liked them immediately. Knowing that Mr. and Mrs. Barnes would be more comfortable talking with the older group, she would seat them with her parents and their friends.

The younger crowd, including Zach, and his sister, Pat, would gather at the other table with Nora, along with Claudia, her husband, Rob, and her good friend, Keith. Nora was also delighted when her mentor, Julia Morgan, had arranged her schedule so that she could join the celebration. The architect was on her way back to San Francisco today from a working weekend at Mr. Hearst's project in San Simeon. Nora had seated Julia next to Zach's sister, Pat, the headmistress of Northfield School in Massachusetts. Both women were devoted to their careers and they would have many things to talk about.

Finally, there were the children. Sally Owens and Freddie Jacklin would sit at Nora's table too. She knew they would likely spend more time on the big swing on the back porch, once they had eaten.

With the weather warm and a light breeze coming off the ocean, at a little after two, everyone stood around the punch bowl. Nora proposed a toast before they sat down to eat. Then she and Mrs. Newsom bustled around the tables, serving the guests. Nora was pleased to see that the group was in high spirits. Judging from the loud chattering and laughing, she knew that her seating arrangements had been a success.

When it was time for coffee, Helen got up to help Lucinda serve dessert. Nora brought out a multi-layered chocolate cake topped with sugared wedding bells that she had ordered from the Carmel Bakery. Her father stood up, thanked everyone for being a part of the celebration, and cut the cake into individual servings. Nora made sure that Sally and Freddie had extra-large helpings.

"Freddie has been wonderful with Maisie's puppies," Rob said to Nora as she came by to pour him a refill of coffee. "Claudia and I appreciate your giving him that dog last fall. Maisie has helped him adjust to our new life as a family."

"I'm glad, Rob," she said. "A boy ought to have a dog to grow up with, and caring for her teaches him responsibility."

Keith sidled up and put his arm around Nora. "Will you come and join my parents and me at the other table? They have something they'd like to say to you."

"As soon as I finish serving this coffee, I'll be right there," she said.

Rob stood up and took the coffeepot from her. "I'll see who needs refills, Nora. Why don't you relax for a minute? You've been on your feet for hours."

Thanking him, she followed Keith. They sat down across from the Prestons.

"We've enjoyed ourselves so much," Cora Preston said. "Your parents and your friends are such delightful people and you've made us feel so welcome. Tomorrow we're taking the train to Los Angeles to visit Lee, but we wanted to properly thank you for saving his life. Having lost our oldest boy in the war, it would have been unbearable to lose our youngest too."

Henry Preston leaned forward. "Miss Nora, if Lee had drowned, his mother and I would have mourned him for the rest of our lives. Granted, he's young and foolish, but he's still our son and we love him. We want to show you our deep gratitude, and we hope you'll accept something from us."

Pulling her up from her seat, Keith said, "Come out front with us. Someone's waiting with a surprise for you."

Arm in arm, and followed by the senior Prestons, Keith and Nora strolled down the side path of her cottage and out to Monte Verde Street. Nora recognized the young man standing there. Pete Quinlan, the owner of the Shamrock Garage, tipped his hat and stepped away from a red Buick two-seater roadster. Pointing at it, he said, "It's only a year old, Nora, and it's in great condition."

Dumbfounded, she asked, "What do you mean?"

Keith took her hand. "My parents used some of the money from Lee's and my trust fund. Lee didn't need it after all. When Mr. Kuster found out that he and his friends wanted to show talking movies, he rejected Lee's offer to invest in his theater."

Keith's father interjected, "We think it's only right that you receive a reward for saving Lee's life. When we heard how eager you've been to learn how to drive, we had Keith tell Pete to start looking for a car. It's all yours, young lady, and here are the keys."

Cora gave Nora a hug. "Thank you from the bottom of my heart. I hope you'll visit us in Charleston one day. I have a little vial of 'Chanel' perfume that I'd like you to have when you come. You see, I always bring some back with me from Paris every year. All the young ladies seem to love it."

"I promise I'll visit, Mrs. Preston," Nora said, "but I still can't believe this wonderful gift."

Just then, Zach walked out to join them. He said, "Keith shared his big secret with me, Nora. I knew nothing would make you happier than driving yourself around Carmel village while you cover your news stories for the *Pine Cone*."

Nora's face glowed with excitement. "That's true, but it's getting too dark for me to drive it now. Come by tomorrow after work, will you, Keith? We'll take it out to Carmel Point for a spin. Now, let's all go back inside and celebrate. My father brought me some new Dixieland jazz records that I can put on the Victrola. I know how much you love that music, Keith Preston."

Giving her a peck on the cheek, he whispered, "I may even get you to dance the fox trot!"

AUTHOR'S NOTE

Murder Takes the Stage and its prequel, Murder in the Pines, were conceived and intended as works of fiction. Most of the characters portrayed in the novels are fictitious, although they have been cast among real persons who lived during those times.

I have fictitiously assigned Julia Morgan, the first woman to practice architecture in California, the role of friend and mentor to my protagonist, Nora Finnegan, all the while acknowledging Miss Morgan's outstanding works: Hearst Castle in San Simeon, and Asilomar in Pacific Grove.

The underlying thread running through Murder Takes the Stage is the presence of theater art in Carmel-By-The-Sea. I am very impressed with the continued existence of the 102-year-old outdoor Forest Theater. It qualifies as California's oldest, open-air community playhouse. The first play performed there took place on the evening of July 9, 1910. Many illustrious Carmelites have been associated with the Forest Theater's early beginnings. Among them are Herbert Heron, Mary Austin, George Sterling, Perry Newberry, Fred Bechdolt, Joseph W. Hand and Michael Williams.

Coinciding with the paving of Ocean Avenue in 1922, Carmel's elected Board of Trustees appointed five individuals to the town's first Planning Commission. They included Doctor Alfred E. Burton, the group's chairman, prominent California architect, Charles Sumner Greene, Carmel Club of Arts and Crafts members, Susan Creighton Porter and Jessie Arms Botke, and local contractor, Thomas B. Reardon. They were charged with providing review and guidance as Carmel entered a major phase of building construction along Ocean Avenue's commercial district. The Commission members were active participants in transforming the village from simple, wood-framed structures into buildings that popularized the Tudor and Spanish Revival styles. One of the prime examples of the new architectural design was Edward Kuster's 1924 Theatre of the Golden Bough. Carmel had been launched. The town saw an upsurge of visitors. The theater arts played a major role then, as now, in making Carmel-By-The-Sea a destination.

A final note. The tin lantern, whose image appears on the previous page, was used in the book by Nora Finnegan and her fellow residents to navigate Carmel's unlit streets at night. It was devised originally by local playwright Bertha Newberry, the wife of journalist and city activist, Perry Newberry. Bertha's lantern consisted of a perforated tin can with a wire handle that held a lighted candle inside. The lanterns have disappeared. The unlit streets have not.

NORA FINNEGAN'S CARMEL

Some of the buildings, structures and locales that existed at the time of the novel can be identified today. To locate them, the reader can refer to the captions below the following photographs.

The outdoor Forest Theater on Mountain View Avenue as seen from the stage. (Chapter One)

A neighborhood milk shrine on the west side of Lincoln Street between Fifth and Sixth Avenues in front of Carmel Heritage's First Murphy House. (Chapter Five)

Abalone League softball field, Carmel Point, 1920s. View toward southwest. Unpaved San Antonio Avenue in foreground. (Chapter Six)

Carmel Arts and Crafts Clubhouse, 1907, current site of the Circle Theater. Located on east side of Casanova Street between Eighth and Ninth Avenues. (Chapter Eleven)

Carmel's 1922 post office, City Hall and police station on west side of Dolores Street between Ocean and Seventh Avenues. (Chapter Twenty Two)

Ruth Kuster's Carmel Weavers Studio at southwest corner of Ocean Avenue and Dolores Street in 1922. (Chapter Twenty Two)

Interior of Carmel Weavers Studio. Expert weaver Ruth Kuster at the loom. (Chapter Twenty Two)

In 1923, Carmel Weavers Studio moved west down Ocean Avenue to double as a ticket office for Edward Kuster's Theatre of the Golden Bough in the background.

ACKNOWLEDGEMENTS

There is no adequate way to thank those who knowingly and unknowingly helped me write *Murder Takes the Stage*. I confess that their hidden talents permeate throughout the book. Without question, the information culled from the City of Carmel-By-The-Sea's Building Permit Files and the historical archives of the Local History Room of the Harrison Memorial Library were invaluable as background material. My thanks go to librarian, Ashlee Wright, for her assistance with materials and photographs. In particular, I want to also give credit to the Master's Thesis by Morgan Evans Stock entitled The Carmel Theatre from 1910-1935, and published in 1952 by Stanford University. It was an excellent source of information, as were Sharron Lee Hale's *A Tribute to Yesterday*, and California Department of Parks and Recreation publications for Point Lobos State Reserve.

My editor, Jacqueline Buie, and book designer, Dorothy Foglia, both provided expert guidance with suggestions and recommendations that resulted in a much better work. Nora Finnegan's image on the book's cover, which now has taken on a virtual life, was created by Kay Holz for my first book, *Murder in the Pines,* and continues to dominate the cover of this book. Deepest thanks go to Kay, who lives in Carmel, and also to Gayle Ortiz, my friend of many years in Capitola, for their insightful comments after reading my original draft. They have made my book a much better story. Finally, I want to acknowledge my husband, Tony, for his support. He has been a constant advisor throughout the process.